Liliana

Book 1, The Liliana Series

by

Neva Squires-Rodriguez

Vanilla Heart Publishing

Liliana
Book 1, The Liliana Series
by Neva Squires-Rodriguez

Copyright 2014 Neva Squires-Rodriguez

Published by: Vanilla Heart Publishing
www.VanillaHeartBookAndAuthors.com
10121 Evergreen Way, 25-156
Everett, WA 98204 USA

This book is a work of fiction. Names, characters, places, and incidents are either the product of the author's imagination or are used fictitiously, and any resemblance to places, events, or persons living or dead is purely coincidental.

ISBN-13: 978-0692307199 ISBN-10: 0692307192

10 9 8 7 6 5 4 3 2 1 First Edition

First Printing, October 2014
Printed in the United States of America

Liliana

Book 1, The Liliana Series

by

Neva Squires-Rodriguez

Table of Contents

Acknowledgements

Book Club Discussion Starters

Bonus Preview
In Too Deep

Neva Squires-Rodriguez
Author Bio and Photo

Acknowledgements

First and foremost, I would like to thank God for giving me the strength that I needed in finishing this book. Without You, I would still be looking for direction in my life. Thank you for bringing me into "Pastor Choco's" (Wilfredo De Jesus's) church and showing me where the path was that I had lost sight of for so long.

A special thanks to my Mother and Father for sharing in my happiness with every step that I've made toward my goals. To my four children, I thank you for picking up extra responsibilities, like cleaning up your room, throwing out the garbage and listening to mommy rave with requests that she made several times, because she forgot whether she ever asked you to do them. To my husband for being my rock in your own special way. You are one in a million and without you, I wouldn't be the person that I am today. To my numerous friends on social media, this one's for you, thank you for inspiring me with your words, your quotes, your jokes and your continuous positive life outlook whether you felt it as positive or not, your words helped move me forward on my own journey. Thank you to Vanilla Heart Publishing for giving me the chance that I needed to get my name out there, I greatly appreciate the opportunity that you've given me. A special thanks to Tamara, Chelle, Kimberlee and Stephanie who guided me in my quest to get my first novel published.

Do you believe in the spirit world? I do and for that reason, I'd also like to give a special thanks to my angels on the other side. To my grandmother Yolanda, I know that you would have loved this story. How I wish you were still here with me to experience the joy that I am feeling right now. To Grandpa Augie, thank you for the persistence that you have taught me. I am forever indebted to you for the many things that you have done for me throughout my life. Thank you for persuading me to finish this book up, even if you were on the other side when you did it. To my Great Grandpa Wade, without you I wouldn't be here today. To Great Grandma Eula, your positive attitude and general love for life has made me at least a quarter of the person I am today. You all are my definition of excellence. I would also like to thank my old friend, Sokari Aton, I owe so much of my faith to you buddy. To all of you, I can still hear your voices, your encouraging words and fell your presence in my own life. For this I owe you whatever success this book may bring my way.

Prologue

The sound of a single gunshot rings through my mind every time I think of her. The sound reminds me of the second that I sat helplessly in my mother's car after her life unexpectedly came to an end. My mind replays those last few moments of the life that I shared with her, as I sit in the backseat of a taxi on my way to the airport, where I will begin a new life in a country that I do not know. At the time I didn't know that very second would be the second that would change my life forever.

Chapter One

It was a Friday night when it happened. My mother was taking me to my aunt's house so that she could go to a nightclub with some of her old friends. She didn't go out very often, so this was a big deal to her. I was thirteen, nearly fourteen years old, and I didn't think that I needed a babysitter. My mother, on the other hand, didn't ever leave me alone. She said that it wasn't that she didn't trust me, she didn't trust other people. Our neighbors were robbed the week before, so I supposed that she was right.

My father and mother were never married. They lived together until I was three. That was the year that he was deported to South America. My mother told me that when it happened, she was glad that it did. She had been trying to get out of the relationship with him since I was born. She said that he was very jealous and if she so much as said "hello" to another man in front of him, he would beat her when they came back home.

My mother was very pretty, and as I began to get older, all of her friends told me that I looked just like her. At first it was embarrassing to me, but after a while I could clearly see the resemblance between us. She had medium length light brown hair and baby blue eyes. She was just an inch taller than me at five foot three. My aunt agreed that I looked more like my mom, but with my father's features and slightly darker hair. My skin was just a little darker then hers and my nose was round, where hers was thin and long.

Liliana

My mom may have been petite, but she was quite the fighter. Ever since my father was deported she'd taken Tae-Kwon-Do classes to protect herself in case he ever tried to come back. She tried to get me involved in Tae-Kwon-Do, too, but I showed no interest in the sport. It would be a waste of money to push me into it. Fighting was the last thing on my mind.

I had just graduated from eighth grade and was excited about starting high school in the fall. I had no enemies at school or in the neighborhood that we lived in. Now, as I sit in the backseat of a cab, on my way to a land that I know nothing about, I feel like I should have taken the classes.

Chapter Two

When my father was deported, he wanted my mother to come and live with him. Back in Colombia, he was able to find a job as a gardener working for some rich family that he worked for years ago, before he came to the United States with my mother. She refused to take me back there, even to visit, out of fear that he wouldn't let her leave. He became really upset with her and called repeatedly to threaten her life if she didn't do what he wanted, so she cancelled our phone service and moved across town to be safe.

My aunt, although she was my father's sister, supported my mother leaving him. This was interesting because she'd never supported their relationship. To her, my mother was a "gringa," or a "white girl." She was resentful toward my mother at first because it was her decision to leave Colombia, but she'd accepted my mother as a friend in the long run, because of me.

My aunt told me when I was about seven that my father had gotten married. He was living with a woman in Colombia for just a few months when she became pregnant. My father, being the man that he was found out that she was pregnant and tried to leave the country. Her family had other plans and forced him to marry her, stopping him after he traveled nearly six hours in an attempt to cross the border and flee into Ecuador. Supposedly, the family gave them a house to live in, because my dad had no money, and he'd agreed to stay. He had trouble finding work and gambled away the measly earnings he did make doing gardening work before he was fired for some unknown reason.

I had been a Daddy's Girl while he was here, so it was hard for me to relate to my mother when she talked about him. My mother tried not to discuss too many things about him with me. She said she was trying to protect me, and sometimes I hated her for that. Here I was, this little girl that didn't know anything about her father, except that I had his last name. I was constantly ridiculed at school for having a "Spanish" last name and not actually knowing how to speak the language.

My mother destroyed every picture she had of him and my aunt only had a few pictures of him from when they were children. In the beginning, Aunt Maria would let me talk to him on the phone while she was babysitting me. She told me to promise not to tell my mother that I had talked with him or I wouldn't be able to come back to her house. I never dared to mention anything about our little secret to my mother. Aunt Maria was my father's sister and she was the only person that my mother trusted enough to babysit me.

My mom didn't have any family of her own. Her parents had died when she was ten years old, leaving her to grow up in an orphanage, where she was later assigned to a foster family that introduced Christianity to her. Mom had even traveled to other countries to help spread the word of Jesus. She was hesitant each time she left me with my aunt, as though she knew she had something up her sleeve.

Aunt Maria has six kids, and if you ask me, I was doing her a favor by going to her house while my mother went out. Aunt Maria was this short chunky woman who always had something to complain about. She was loud and she cursed a lot. My mother told me that Maria and my father didn't look anything alike because they had two different fathers. My grandmother only had the two of them and passed away when my father was eighteen. Because she was only fourteen at the time, Aunt Maria was left in my father's care.

My mother had mentioned to me that if she ever died, she didn't know what would happen to me. She said that she would like for me to live with one of her old friends, Grace Hooper. Grace didn't have any kids and lived alone in a two bedroom apartment on the North Side. Apparently my mom never put a plan in place, which is why I sit in the back of a cab on my way to the airport.

Chapter Three

On that life-changing Friday night, Mom was running late as she tried to figure out which outfit to wear. I lay across her bed brushing my long brownish-blonde hair, looking at my eighth grade class graduation picture. I was ready to go, but I didn't rush my mother because I was in no hurry to go to my aunt's house. I lay there imagining the hours of screaming I had to look forward to, while I attempted to refocus my energy on the picture of my classmates. Ten minutes later, my mother finally decided on a navy blue sweater with a pair of black jeans. My mother sighed in discouragement as she grabbed her keys from the top of the dresser. I grabbed my own keys, just in case she lost hers and we weren't able to get back in the house. Finally, we were ready to leave and we headed out to the car.

"I can't believe how windy it is." My mother said, obviously trying to hold a conversation.

It was dark and the wind was loud as it blew around us. Garbage was flying around in the street as we walked to her car. Somewhere down the street a dog began to bark, as if it was giving us a warning that something bad was about to happen.

"Well you know this is Chicago weather, Mom." I replied under my breath.

My mother smirked at me and we climbed into the car. It was nearly the end of summer, but the wind whipped around as if we were going to have a tornado.

I popped my CD in and we drove in silence as we listened to the music. The song that played was by a hip hop artist that I knew my mother didn't like. I could see the sullen expression on my mother's face as she tried to remain in a good mood. I couldn't help myself as I tried to irritate her. I was upset that she was going out. Why couldn't she spend more time with me? I knew that she didn't go out often and I knew that I wasn't supposed to say anything to spoil her night. I just wanted more of her time I guess and I really didn't know how to show her that, aside from being a brat.

My mother had just bought this car, a navy blue Ford Mustang that was a few years old, a week ago. She said it still ran like new. That's probably the reason she was going out, I thought. She wanted to show it off to her friends. I guess that maybe I would have liked to show it off, too. I thought about how much I loved riding in my mother's "new" car. It was so shiny and sleek that I felt like I was worth a million bucks in it.

I noticed teenage boys turning their heads as we drove past them, while they waited at the bus stop. I thought of waving at a few, but I was too shy to do that. I had never had a boyfriend because I agreed with my mom when she said I was too young to date. My mother joked with me as a boy said hello, in passing, and acted like she did not believe me when I said that they were just friends. The truth of the matter was, that I had never even kissed a boy, although I imagined what it would be like to kiss one every day of my life.

I sighed as I thought of that and leaned against the side of the door, staring at skyscraper after skyscraper until we stopped at a red light. I remember looking around and thinking of how quiet the street was. We were so close to the lake, the wind blew sand across the streets. I was glad that my window was closed. My mother liked to drive with her window open, and she stared right into the wind as it blew. Mother was an occasional smoker and this was one of those nights.

I remember looking over at Mom and wondering if we had made a wrong turn. She stared intently ahead of her as she waited for the green light. I knew that she was thinking about how her night would go. I wished at that very moment she hadn't decided to go out and that I could have stayed home and watched my favorite shows on television. I knew that I wouldn't be able to pay any attention to them at my aunt's house. That was if I was allowed to change the channel from her favorite novella, I thought. At that moment I was snapped back to reality.

"Give me your purse!" I heard a man scream.

I froze and looked over at the man. He stood at my mother's window with a gun pointed to her head, without seeing me. She looked at me in shock as she reached over to my side of the car and slowly picked up her purse from the floor. Her expression said a million words. She seemed hesitant as she lifted her purse. I could feel my heart begin to pound hard enough that it felt like it was going to jump right out of my chest. She handed the purse to the man ever so slowly. In the process I felt her cell phone fall down by my feet and covered it with my foot to hide it from him. I began to breathe heavily. I was sure that he had seen me.

He wore a black ski mask with black gloves. I noticed the brand, an unrecognizable name on a tag as he took the purse from my mother. I stared at his dark brown eyes peering out nervously, through the eye holes in his mask. His voice sounded young and I wondered if he was even that much older than me. He didn't have an accent, but I knew from the way that he pronounced his words, he wasn't from Chicago.

The man ordered my mother out of the car. I knew my mother thought that she could take him down. I grabbed her hand to try to stop her. She glanced at me as she tapped my hand, as if to tell me that it would be okay. I glanced over at her as she seemed to size him up and shot me an expression that worried me. That expression was the same one that she gave me when she was going to one of her competitions. I shook my head at her as she complied with him and slowly began to get out of the car. As soon as she had both feet outside of the car "Boom," he shot her right in the head. Her body fell to the ground and I noticed that blood began to quickly ooze from her head.

"No!" I screamed in disbelief.

I tried to scream out for help but grasped my throat instead - no words would come out. Tears flooded my face. The man turned the gun on me, but for whatever reason decided not to shoot. I thought that maybe it was because he realized how young I was. I clutched the door handle as if it would save me, the same way I did when my mother was cutting through traffic in the morning rush hour. I looked up and saw a person's head quickly move back from a window of an apartment building at the corner of the block.

I looked at the robber in disgust. I was afraid for my life, but at the same time I wanted to show him that I was furious. He had taken my mother away from me. Our eyes held together for a moment. I swore to myself that I would never forget those eyes. They seemed to pierce me with their sharp definition. The next thing I knew, he got in the car and tried to drive it away, not giving a second thought to me as I sat beside him in the passenger seat.

I gripped the door hard, tears fell from my eyes and I let out a scared moan. I guess he didn't realize that the car was a stick shift and he crashed it into a dumpster in a nearby alley. He turned the gun on me again but didn't shoot. I swallowed my breath and it seemed to lodge within my chest. He didn't say a word to me. It was as though by pointing the gun at me he knew that I would remain quiet.

The sirens got louder, and the man jumped out of the car and ran down the alley. I saw him get into a dark car with someone else as they hit the gas to drive off. I grabbed the cell phone from under my foot and somehow managed to dial 9-1-1 with my hands shaking vigorously. I looked at the phone for a moment and wondered why no one was answering. I remembered a moment later that I forgot to hit the send key. Where was the send key? I couldn't figure it out.

The moment was filled with confusion and instead of trying the call again I dropped the phone and struggled to get my door open. When I finally succeeded I ran down the alley, going back to my mother, who lay in the street in a pool of blood. I quickly fell to the ground beside her. I tried to find a way to stop the bleeding but I couldn't. Her hair was drenched in blood and I couldn't figure out where the bullet had hit.

My hands began to feel sticky with her blood and my clothing became covered in it as well. The blood seemed to wake me up to reality and at that moment I knew my darkest fear had become my reality as I looked into my mother's foggy blue eyes, which remained open without a single blink. I had lost my mother. Would I become an orphan I wondered? I lay my head against her chest but quickly lifted it and tried once again to save her. I knew within my heart that she was dead, but I still tried, shaking her furiously. How could that man take my mother from me? Why wasn't someone coming to help me? It seemed to take hours before the sirens reached me.

Two paramedics ran to my mother's side. One told me to step aside as he quickly hoisted my mother on a stretcher and lifted it into a red and white ambulance. I looked back at where she had been laying on the ground just moments before, the ground still covered in blood, our car crashed nearby as two police cars approached the scene. One of the paramedics waved at the police offers, indicating that we were ready to go, while the other ushered me into the ambulance with my mother. I could hear the beating of my heart pounding against my chest as my mind replayed the sound of the gunshot over and over again.

When I climbed into the back of the ambulance I noticed that the first paramedic was holding my mother's wrist and shaking his head. The other, a woman, looked at me sympathetically and asked me my name, my age and for someone they could call. My voice shook as I told her my name.

"Lil-i-ana," I said slowly, concentrating on the pronunciation of my own name and desperately trying to remember my aunt's phone number.

Finally the numbers came into my head and I spit them out quickly, forgetting each one as I spoke. My heart seemed to sink deeper and deeper into my soul with every breath and I could not think of anything I wanted more than for my mother to come back to life. I reached out for her and felt like her soul was looking down at me. I shook as I thought I heard her tell me that everything was going to be alright. I let my hand drop in fear and looked helplessly to the female paramedic who was giving a third paramedic up front my aunt's phone number. She moved closer to me when she was done and put her arm around me. I began to sob and turned to her as if she was family, crying into her shoulder and sinking deeper and deeper into her grasp.

When we arrived at the hospital the paramedics in the front jumped out and ran to the back to open the doors for us. When they did I saw several staff members waiting at the curb. They stood still as though they were hesitant to move, one even opened his mouth as if he wanted to ask a question, but closed it when he saw me and moved quickly toward my mother. Somewhere in the back of my mind, I thought maybe, just maybe, they could still do something to save her. The paramedics took her straight to the emergency room. I followed behind slowly, with the help of the female paramedic.

As we entered the waiting room I noticed that there was a police officer seated nearby. The paramedic who drove the ambulance handed me a t-shirt with their company's logo on it to change into. Soon I discovered that the police officer was waiting to question me as one of the other paramedics nodded at him and then at me. He came over and introduced himself. His words sounded blurred together as he began to speak. I had trouble focusing on what he was saying and a nurse came over and handed me a bottle of water. My hands shook as I opened it and raised it to my mouth, but the water helped me regain my focus.

I immediately noticed his name tag said Officer Rogers and tried to smile as I looked up at him. The female paramedic left my side, leaving me alone with the officer. He pressed me for as much information as he could get. I stood there staring at him, trying my best to decipher what he was saying. Some of his questions confused me. I knew what he must have been asking, but my only concern was where the paramedics had taken my mother.

Focus. Lily, I thought to myself and finally broke down in tears telling him that all I could remember was that he had dark brown eyes and was wearing all black. I paused for a moment and told him about the getaway car, but was upset with myself that I could not remember anything about it. "It drove away quickly." I managed to say slowly as I gazed into his disappointed eyes. "It all happened so fast."

I cried and questioned myself as to why I didn't notice more about the man. I had no idea how tall he was, or how much he might have weighed. Why hadn't I taken he time to notice that? All that I had been thinking about was the stupid cell phone I hid under my foot. Why hadn't I noticed the direction that he had come from or what direction he had run to?

"Liliana!" A woman exclaimed.

I looked up to see Aunt Maria running down the hallway with her two oldest children. She grabbed me and held me in her arms while I cried. She pushed me away for a moment as she looked me in the eyes, biting down on her lip as she began to speak.

"Baby, your mother didn't make it." She said.

I sobbed and tried desperately to catch my breath. Her kids looked at me in horror as though they couldn't understand why I was so upset.

What else could I do? I felt my mother's life slipping further and further away from me. My mother was gone! She was gone! Aunt Maria's eight year old daughter, Maritza, stroked my leg.

"Lily, do you want some candy?" She asked.

No, I want my mother! I wanted to scream, but I could not get the words to come out of my mouth. I knew deep in my heart that she was only trying to make me feel better. She stood next to me eating a bag of Skittles one by one, obviously enjoying the taste of each flavor. I stared blankly at her for a moment in disgust. She knew my mother, how could she possibly be enjoying a bag of candy at a time like this?

A doctor came out of a room nearby and introduced himself to my aunt and me as Dr. Roy. He told us to follow him so that we could say our goodbyes. We heard a crash nearby as we began to walk. We looked over only to see that my aunt's son had knocked over a lamp from the table. Although he was nearly twelve years old, he was a klutz.

"I'll clean that up." A nurse said lightly, touching my aunt's arm so that she wouldn't yell at her son. Dr. Roy looked at my aunt's two children sternly, but hesitantly allowed them to come with us.

We followed Dr. Roy down a long white hallway and turned into a small room, just past a nurse's station. My aunt's son Rodolfo Jr. gasped and turned away the moment we entered the room. My mother's hair was still covered with blood and her skin looked pale. I could not say anything. I stood in silence, not even thinking about anything.

Liliana

At that point the realization still had not sunk into my brain, that my mother, my only real family, was dead. Never would I feel her tender touch again. Never would I have her to argue with again. Suddenly everything hit me and my mind began to fill with regrets. Why hadn't I talked more with her this evening? Why hadn't I told her that she couldn't go out tonight, or rather that I didn't want her to?

Maritza broke the silence and asked the doctor why my mother's skin was pale. He looked from her to my aunt and then slowly to the door. My aunt looked horrified for a moment before nodding to the doctor. He took Maritza and Rodolfo Jr. to the doorway and called for a nurse to take them to the waiting area. She placed a hand against each of their backs, ushering them down the hallway and explaining death to the two as one would to a child. I continued to stare at my mother as my aunt took my mother's hand in hers, tears flowing down her cheeks, though she remained quiet.

Just then a different nurse came to the room and asked Aunt Maria to tell me to say my goodbyes because they had to take my mother's body to the morgue. The nurse, I thought, could have been more understanding. She made it obvious that she was looking at the clock on the wall, just to the left of my head. I could hear the clock ticking loudly in the background and couldn't focus on anything but the sounds of the hands as they moved.

"It's not good for her to see this." The nurse said quietly to my aunt, motioning at the doorway.

Aunt Maria nodded at me. She held my hand as we stared at my mother's lifeless body. I wanted to embrace my mother and stay the entire night with her. I searched for words to say to my mother, but I didn't know what to say. I remembered just last month I had complained about a movie that she had bought for me as a birthday gift. I had gone on about it for a week, ranting and raving every time we were near each other. I wanted to tell her that I was sorry for everything and that I loved the movie, but instead as my lips finally parted and I pulled words from my dry throat I choked. "You can take her." I said, telling myself that somehow, my mother knew what I was thinking.

I wanted to throw myself at her bed as the nurse wheeled it away. I felt like I should be saying or doing more. I felt like I was reacting to the whole situation in the wrong way. I tried to tell myself that what I should be thinking about was my mother and what had happened, how she would be thinking and what she would have wanted. Instead my only thoughts were for myself. What would happen to me and where was I going to go?

My mother had no family. She was an only child and her parents were dead! No sisters, brothers, uncles or aunts. I didn't know any of her friend's phone numbers, though I was sure that I would be able to find them on her cell phone. My mother had lived in an orphanage until she met my father, and then they had me. Suddenly I froze.

"Oh no," I thought to myself. Was this what was going to happen to me?

Was I going to become an orphan as well? There was my father, who was in Colombia, but I didn't want to live with him, his wife and my replacement, his new kid. I imagined the kid had to be at least seven or eight by now. I thought about his sister, my Aunt Maria and her husband. I didn't think they would take me in. They already had six kids of their own and lived in a two bedroom apartment with three sets of bunk beds in one room. I knew they were hardly cutting it on my uncle's salary as a dishwasher at the Congress Hotel downtown. Then again, I thought to myself, what difference would one extra kid make? I let out a shallow breath as my aunt looked over and came to me and embraced me, holding my head to her shoulder.

I grabbed onto her tightly and cried into her shoulder.

"What's going to happen now?" I muttered.

Aunt Maria rubbed my back but she cried, too. She nodded her head. "Your mother was a great woman Liliana," she managed to say in between tears, rubbing my back faster as she spoke. "Never forget how wonderful she was."

I felt worse than ever. I would never see my mother's beautiful face again and here I was thinking about where I was going to live, while my aunt was obviously thinking about my sweet mother.

Liliana

"Hello, my name is Officer Rogers." A male voice quietly interrupted.

I looked up to see that it was the police officer from earlier.

"Can I have a word with you?" The officer asked my aunt.

She looked to me for approval and I shrugged my thin shoulders, as I gazed away from the two of them. I felt as though the police officer studied my expression to see if I had remembered anything else. They walked out a few steps into the hallway. I glanced back at them, noticing that they moved to a spot where I could still see them. They were out of ear shot as they spoke quietly. I watched the two talking as they periodically glanced over at me.

The officer talked for at least five minutes, before he started motioning with his hands as he spoke. My aunt gave a quick response and shook her head. This went on for quite some time, the officer would talk and then my aunt would shake her head as the officer began to jot in his notebook what she was saying. Then finally my aunt nodded after something that he said and I could read her lips as she said *Colombia*.

Chapter Four

I stood frozen with horror. I didn't know my father, how could they expect me to live with him? How would I communicate with the people there? I waited in anticipation for my aunt to come back over and let me know what was going on. I couldn't help but feel afraid, alone, and in a jumble of grief. Could I ever love my father like I loved my mother? Could I run away and find an orphanage that would take me in and did I really want to be there if I did? I remembered my mom telling me horrible stories of her time in a local girls' home, where she fought with other girls for her own possessions and always worried that they would jump her the moment that she let her guard down. I argued with these thoughts in my head until my aunt came back with the police officer.

"Mija, you are going to have to go live with your father in Colombia." My aunt quickly said, nodding as if to answer any questions that I had.

I shook my head and stepped away from her as she tried to touch my arm.

"No, I can't Maria." I blatantly said.

My aunt looked at me in shock. This was the first time I had called her by her first name and I knew that she considered that to be disrespectful. I didn't mean to say it like that, I thought to myself.

"Honey, you must," she said, as if she was still trying to convince herself. "Your Papi will take good care of you. I can't take you in. I just can't. He loves you." She patted my shoulder, still showing signs that she was upset with me as the police officer led us out the door.

"I'll be right behind you," Officer Rogers said quietly to my aunt as she gathered her kids and exited the hospital.

We climbed into her vehicle, my hands still trembling as I fastened my seat belt. The police officer followed us all back to my house – Mom's house. My aunt and cousins sat in silence. My thoughts moved on to what to bring from home; moving my life to a place I'd never known.

When we arrived, the police officer told me to pack no more than one suitcase and a carryon bag with my belongings. I was angry that my life was being tossed around and shrugged as I walked past him. I turned only to tell the police officer and my aunt that I didn't want to stay for my mother's service... that I wanted to get away from all the people that didn't want me in their lives as soon as I could.

I would regret my stubbornness for years to come, but at that moment I wanted to get my point across. My aunt used the police officer's cell phone to call my father in Colombia with her calling card. She spoke quickly in Spanish, asking the neighbor nearest my father's house who had the only phone, to go and get him as tears dripped from her eyes.

While she waited for him to come to the phone, she glanced over at me. I could only look away. I was the one who was hurt. She had no reason to be sad. She ended the call telling him the officer would call him with my flight arrangements the following day, and then looked down at her lap as she sat inside of the car.

My aunt asked the officer, as she got out of the car, if she could come again at a later time to take out the rest of my mother's things and possibly have them sent to me. Then she asked him if he knew of a charity that she could donate her clothes and furniture to.

Oh give me a break! I wanted to choke my aunt! I couldn't believe that she was thinking of what charity to donate all Mom's things to while I was going to pack my whole life away. Didn't she know that these things were priceless and that my mom had worked so hard for them? I couldn't believe that she was discussing what to do with the things right in front of me. No one was even discussing where they would bury her or when the funeral would be held yet. When would they do that, I wondered? Was that not as important to them as her belongings were? What about me? Why were they so quick to decide that they would send me to Colombia? No one even bothered to ask me what I wanted to do. I wanted to leave, to run, and to do anything to get away from everyone.

I could feel my resentment toward my aunt growing. I glared at her as she walked over and stood at the doorway of our home. When I finally reached into my pocket to pull out my keys, I trembled as I opened the lock. The house was just as we had left it, the entrance still smelling of my mother's perfume. I breathed it in, imagining for a moment that my mother was there with me. My aunt touched my small trembling shoulder.

"Liliana, just take what you need."

I fumed as Rodolfo Jr. and Maritza came inside, plopped down on the sofa and turned on the television as if nothing had happened. I wanted to tell them to go wait in the car, but instead I went to the hallway closet and grabbed my mother's largest suitcase and a duffel bag and took them into my room, shutting the door behind me. I heard the officer begin to question my aunt about strange people that my mother might have talked about, mentioning one in particular as he picked up a letter that had come in the mail from Colombia. I tuned their voices out and sprawled out across my bed for the last time. I cried and cried, until I made myself realize what I was crying about. I couldn't help thinking my mother was too young to die. Then I asked myself, if there was really a designated age to die? I told myself that accidents happened in death just as they did in birth. I thought of Aunt Maria's son Rodolfo Jr. and how my mother had always privately told me that he was an accident. Was I an accident, I wondered?

I forced myself to get up and go to my closet. I filled my suitcase with my clothes, socks, shoes, bras and panties. I put my picture album and a small framed picture of my mother on top of the clothes and leaned on the suitcase until it closed. Then I looked at the duffel bag, wondering what I could put in it. I had never been on a plane before, much less out of the country. I did have a passport and knew that I would need it. I remembered hearing my Aunt telling the officer about it. I shook my head as I put it in the bag. I looked around my room one last time. There was nothing left that I wanted to keep or that would fit in the bag. I took the bag to the door of my room, reluctantly calling out that I was ready to leave.

I started to leave the room, but then turned back and grabbed her favorite picture of the two of us at my graduation. A tear fell from my eye as I remembered how happy she was at that very moment. I talked to the room as if my mother was standing in it. "I'm going to miss you, Mom." I said and then turned and walked out toward the living room.

Rodolfo Jr. grabbed my suitcase and started to lug it to the front door. The police officer stood up and told him that he would carry it the rest of the way. Rodolfo turned to me.

"Lily, are you sure that you didn't forget anything?" He said in a sarcastic tone.

He and I always had joked around because we were so close in age, but this time I said nothing to him and he turned away and looked down because he knew that he had said something wrong. My aunt took the keys from me and locked the door as soon as we stepped out.

"Lily," she turned and said to me. "I know this hard for you. It's hard for all of us. I love you like a daughter, but I can't take you in. Please understand that."

Her bottom lip trembled furiously when she was done speaking. I watched it as it shook without blinking my eye. She broke down in tears seconds later and hugged me. I could only push her away and nod. Right now, it was not logical for everyone to think that I would be ok, that I didn't have stronger feelings than theirs or that I could forgive anyone for their actions.

I stayed with my aunt for a week. That's how long it took for the police department to rush my paperwork to Colombia and back for my transport. Everyone spoke about it as though my life was as easy to transfer to Colombia as my suitcase was. During that week, my aunt decided to have my mom cremated and planned to scatter her ashes across Lake Michigan, despite my pleas to have her buried at a cemetery. I wanted to be able to come back and visit my mother one day. She had never said which burial method she preferred, but I was sure that she didn't want to be scattered in the lake. The day finally came that Aunt Maria had to make a decision. She borrowed money from my uncle's family to bury her.

My aunt's apartment was crowded and I felt as though I never had a moment to myself while I was there. Even when I was taking a shower, one of the smaller kids had to run in and use the bathroom every five minutes. There was no lock, so I learned to take showers as quickly as possible. I did not have my own bed to sleep in while I was there and slept on the sofa, scared to move because of all the cockroaches that were in the apartment. There were some moments that I actually looking forward to going to stay with my father in Colombia.

My aunt had spoken with him and told me that I would have my own room, which I had now learned to appreciate and miss. She also mentioned that I would need to help out while I was there, though she never said what it was that I'd need to do, which I found odd. The night before I left as I was sleeping Rodolfo woke me up just as I had finally managed to fall asleep.

"Lily, Lily," he said shaking me.

"What?" I said loudly.

"Be quiet," he replied, glancing around the room to make sure that no one heard us. "I heard my mom talking to your father on the phone today. Lily, be careful when you go there," he said, before going back to his room.

I stared at the wall in the dark. Great, this was just what I needed. Now I felt overwhelmingly worried and did not fall asleep again that night. In the morning my aunt called a cab and told me to get ready. We left her house before anyone woke up. My aunt told me to behave myself when I visited with my father, making it sound like I would be coming back. I attempted a smile and nodded, but that was all she told me.

I felt that I was being auctioned off to whoever would take me, the price not important to anyone but myself. I wanted my mother back. Then, and now, as I sat in the back seat of the taxi cab on my way to the airport with my aunt, suitcase in hand and memories left behind.

She didn't even look at me or hug me as I entered the airport to board the plane. She walked with me as far as the metal detectors, and then handed me off to an airport agent that would walk me to my terminal, but as I walked down the hall to board my plane, I looked back and she was gone.

When I finally made it to my seat, I smiled at the person I sat next to. He was an older man who sat reading a Spanish newspaper over his thick framed glasses. I looked around and noticed that most people on the plane, including the flight attendant, looked like they might be Colombian. The flight attendant winked at me as she stood at the front of the plane giving directions on the seatbelts and landing gear in Spanish before it was played on the overhead speakers in English.

I turned and saw a couple of American teenagers seated at the back of the plane. They appeared to be aloof from the rest of us, laughing and discussing places that they would visit when they landed. I thought they were so lucky. They were going to Colombia to finish off their summer break perhaps. Maybe even to study for school. They would then each be able to go back to their family and the people that they loved when everything was said and done. I knew they had no idea about how lucky I thought they were and I knew they had no idea how badly I wanted to be them as I sat quietly admiring them. One glanced at me and I immediately turned, pretending I was looking for the flight attendant. As she passed, I asked her where the bathrooms were, but did not move as she motioned to one at the back of the plane.

I sat back in my seat and decided to think of questions to ask my father when I got off the plane. Soon I realized that I had so many questions, I couldn't keep them all in my head and I needed to write them down. I went to the back of the plane to ask one of the American teenagers if they had some paper. The girl I asked was so drunk that she gave me her whole notebook. She and her friend reeked of alcohol.

"Take it. Take it all!" She said and then her head fell back and she let out a big snore.

Perhaps she did that on purpose, I had no idea. I shook my head as the flight attendant caught my eye and smiled.

I shrugged her behavior off and walked back to my seat, sitting down and beginning to write. The plane took off and the captain announced that we would be stopping briefly in Florida, before continuing on to Colombia and that those who were continuing on, could remain on the aircraft. I sighed and continued writing when the plane stabilized itself in the air, I had so many questions that I turned page after page until the notebook was full. I sighed, not realizing that I had so much to ask my father. Soon my eyes began to feel heavy and I fell asleep for the remainder of the flight. I dreamt that my mother held me in her arms and told me that she loved me over and over as she used to when I was younger, as my head toggled around upon landing. I could feel myself actually holding my mother and it felt so good that I didn't want to let go.

I awoke to the flight attendant shaking me lightly. I slowly opened my eyes and noticed the last passenger stepping off the plane. I grabbed my carryon bag and ran after him. When I got to the passageway from the plane, I looked out the windows. Everything looked so beautiful. The grass was bright green. There were birds sitting nearby despite the roaring airplane that was taking off not far away. The birds were so colorful that I felt like I was looking out into a postcard. I smiled as I waited for my father to greet me.

I looked around as I stepped into the waiting area to see if I recognized my father. My aunt had told me he was tall and had dark hair and would be wearing a white t-shirt. I looked around and saw that this description fit just about every male there. I stood by the exit until most of the people had cleared the area, running into the arms of their loved ones. Tears welled up in my eyes. I thought my father had forgotten about me. I looked around to see if there was a payphone. I started to walk towards one when I spotted it to call my aunt collect.

Just as I did, a man with a slender build grabbed me by my arm so hard I thought it would bruise.

"Do you speak Spanish," he asked me.

"No." I replied as my body trembled.

"Good." He said. "I told my wife you were coming, but she doesn't want the kids to know who you are. They don't speak English so it should be ok. If they ever ask you who you are, just tell them you are here to do some work for me."

He quickly began walking, pulling my arm hard as we walked away from the waiting area.

"I'm sorry." I said, as I pulled my arm away to question him. "I don't believe we've met, did my father send you?"

"Father?" He asked.

He glanced around the waiting room and eyed a pretty flight attendant that whispered something to an airport worker standing beside her.

"Yeah, that's a good word." The man said. "Just don't call me Papa, Papi, or even Daddy. If you do the kid's will probably start to think something."

"Excuse me." I replied, throwing my hands to my hips and stamping my foot down hard against the ground.

I looked up at the man that I could now tell I somewhat resembled. His leathery dark skin dripped with sweat as I stood staring at him.

"You're my father!" I exclaimed loudly to him. "How dare you not introduce yourself, after all these years of not even calling to say hello!"

Then it happened. *Bam*! The man now known to me as my father smacked me across my face so hard I stumbled to the side.

"Don't ever talk to me like that again!" He said loudly.

I was stunned. I looked around to see that numerous witnesses were watching us. They had seen him hit me but did nothing. The flight attendant shook her head and quickly began to walk away. Men smirked and went back to what they were doing. The women looked away and continued with their conversations. I was expecting someone to run to my side and scold my father. No one even asked if I was okay. This was the exact moment that I came to the realization of just how different things were here and why my mother had never let me visit him.

I pulled myself together after my father hit me, not because I wanted to, but because there was no other choice. I realized that I was now on his team and that I had to play by his rules. My heart ached with pain, almost more than my face did. I couldn't believe that my father had forgotten that I was once the little girl that ran to greet him when he came home. I rubbed my face as I began to walk alongside him.

"Do you have any bags?" My father asked.

I looked up at him. I turned my head so that he could see the redness in my cheek, which was growing hot and tingled with pain, and nodded. We went to get my bags without saying another word. I had no idea where I was going as I followed his lead and looked up at yellow guide signs that were written in Spanish. My father did not ever apologize to me for hitting me. My mind filled with the questions that I wanted to ask him, but I decided that from what I knew so far about him, I didn't care what the answers were.

I picked up my own suitcase from the conveyor belt and carried it toward him. At this point, I wasn't surprised that he didn't offer to help me and figured that while I was here, I'd be growing some muscles, so why not start now?

"Come on, let's go." He said as he began to walk off.

I followed, struggling with my bags in order to keep up with him. He glanced back at me with an annoyed expression, but did not even offer to hold a bag. He walked out of the airport and I tried to keep up with him as I fought the urge to glance around to observe the area as he walked steps ahead of me through the street. The weather here was much hotter than I expected, it was August and I could tell it was much warmer than ninety degrees. I glanced around at different buildings as we walked. I knew that we were in Riohacha and the city was pretty crowded.

"Do you have a car?" I asked him.

"Yes." He replied grouchily.

Several blocks later he finally stopped walking and opened the trunk of an older model vehicle. He motioned for me to put the bags inside and then we climbed in. I sat down in the front seat, but he told me that I needed to move to the back. I complied, though I was annoyed with him. His seats were plush and comfortable and his car was clean. I touched the red material of the seat which felt velvety and smooth.

"I didn't want to waste gas coming up here." He said suddenly with an angry tone.

I bit my lip as our eyes met in the rearview mirror. He turned on the radio, which aired news in Spanish. He was momentarily quiet as he began to drive through the city. I gazed out the window as I looked at palm trees and women near the side of the road sewing purses and making hats. Everything was beautiful at first, but as we drove out of the city everything quickly changed as I began to see more greenery and cactuses.

"We aren't rich you know and anyways I didn't want you to get used to riding around in a car." He said.

I leaned my head against the windowsill in disappointment. As we drove further I didn't see many cars pass us. I did notice quite a few motorcycles drive by periodically. I couldn't believe that we had left the city so quickly, while he drove incredibly slowly. We passed through areas that looked as though some type of wild life would jump out of the tall grass at us. Finally after half an hour uphill we made it to a neighborhood and turned in. The houses looked pretty deserted, though there was a soccer ball lying in the middle of the street that my father drove around. I assumed that the kids in the area had gone home for the night. Finally, we stopped at a small orange house and three kids ran up to my father and hugged him.

"This is my family." My father said.

The woman who I assumed was his wife eyed me cautiously.

"My wife, Teresa," he said as he nodded at a heavy set woman.

Teresa stared at me intently as he spoke, but said nothing.

"And my children." He finished off as he pointed to each of them. "Madrigal, Enrique Jr., and Nicolas."

I instantaneously felt twitches of jealousy. His children were able to grow up with a mom and a dad, while he left my mother to raise me on her own. His wife had been out on the porch with a magazine but rolled her eyes and went inside the house. The oldest daughter looked like she was about seven or eight, just as I had suspected. My father said something to her in Spanish, telling me in English moments later that she would show me to my room. She motioned for me to follow her as she led me into the house. A smile appeared on her thin face as she waved me in.

Madrigal had big brown eyes and dark skin. She wore a dress with a red jacket. Her socks looked like soccer socks and she wore them halfway up her legs with Mary Jane shoes. Her hair was long and extended just about to her butt, pulled back in a thin braid. When she smiled at me I could tell that half her teeth were missing. I remembered that smile from my own pictures in second grade, though aside from that, I didn't think we looked too much alike.

We walked through the house and down a long hallway where Madrigal took me to a small room without a window. It was the only room in the house that wasn't painted and it smelled of mildew. The room was near the kitchen and looked like it may have been a closet or perhaps a pantry. There were screw holes on the wall that looked like shelves had been removed from it. Had they made this into a bedroom for me I wondered, as I briefly looked in at it? I lugged my bag in and pushed it under the bed.

My father came in just as I did and nodded for Madrigal to leave. She glanced back at me happily as she left the room. My father entered, though the room was hardly big enough for the two of us. His wife stood in the kitchen watching us closely as he did. I felt my body shudder as he began to speak to me. I felt like I already hated him and I hadn't even known him a day yet.

"You better get some sleep tonight. Tomorrow you will be starting your new job."

I looked up at him, analyzing his expression for a moment. Had my father always been this way, I wondered? He must have once been a gentleman for my mother to have loved him. He was a somewhat handsome man with his dark complexion and chiseled face, but his attitude made him look evil as I stared blankly at him. I noticed that his hands looked more feminine than masculine and that he wore no ring on his finger, which I thought was odd. I said nothing to him as he stood in the doorway.

He left the room and turned off the hallway light that divided my room from the kitchen. There was no light in my new room so it was dark. A curtain was hung on my doorway for privacy, but there was no door. I could hear the others talking in the next room, though I had no idea what they were discussing. I sat down in my new bed and felt small hard objects poking at me from under the sheets. I grabbed one and played with it in my hand and realized that the mattress was just a huge pillow case filled with hay. I reached in my bag and took out a sweatshirt to put my head on top of.

I attempted to calm myself as I lay looking up at the ceiling. His neighborhood was fairly quiet and despite the fact that my room was completely dark, I could not fall asleep. In the distance I heard a dog barking and thought of my mother, as I began to cry quietly. I was scared that the others might have heard me, but if they did, no one came to check to see if I was alright. I trembled as I remembered what had happened at the airport. I remembered that as a very small girl, I had looked up to my father. I wondered what had made his feelings toward me change.

I thought of what my father had said about my new job and wondered if this would be temporary work, or if this was a permanent job. When he would enroll me in school? I imagined that he knew how old I was. Surely I wasn't old enough to work. I thought about that for a moment and then realized that my father didn't want to get to know me. I felt my heart tightening. I closed my eyes, but was aware of every small sound around me. Before light even peered in my doorway from the kitchen window the next morning, my father came to wake me up.

"Come on."

He handed me a piece of toast and a container of water as I sat up.

"This is for you to wear on the way to work." He said, handing me an ugly jacket.

I wanted to ask him about school but I was too scared to question him.

His wife was awake and I could see her watching us from the kitchen, her lips pressed together and her bangs blown off to the side. She was far from beautiful. She seemed to have the same attitude as he did as she crinkled up her nose at me. She wore a purple sweatshirt and jeans that did not fit her body well. I wondered if she had been pretty when my father met her.

He handed me my jacket again and told me to put it on. It was cool, not cold enough for a jacket, but I did as I was told. I ate the toast quickly and wiped the sleep from my eyes. He appeared to be aggravated with the amount of time I was taking and grabbed my wrist as he pulled me outside. I breathed heavily to show my aggravation but didn't dare question or talk back to him. He walked me around the side of his car where he took out a maid's uniform wrapped in plastic from the trunk and told me to hold it.

He quickly began giving me directions on how to get to my new job, telling me that I must walk down the partial dirt road by our house for two miles before I would see a gas station and walk toward it, turning on the paved road and would continue walking until I got to a big house, where I would ask for Elena. I smirked. Was he serious? I began to question him but he hushed me and started toward his door. The sun had begun to come up and he shot me an expression that told me that I better start walking, as I left reluctantly on foot.

I stopped to look back at my dad and the house as I walked down the dusty road. I expected to see him on the porch watching me as I left, but my father had already gone back into the house, probably to go back to sleep, I thought. I tried to push the picture of him out of my mind as I turned and began to walk down the dirt road. The neighborhood was bustling at this time. I saw several other people setting out on foot as they said goodbye to their families.

Chapter Five

As I walked, I began to wonder if I was lost. I looked around at the scenery and felt as if I was walking through the middle of the jungle. There were green plants on either side of the seemingly neverending dirt road. Many other people had turned left or right at least a mile before. I wiped my face of sweat. I had already walked at least two hours. Finally in the distance, I saw the gas station. I glanced to the side and saw the paved road that I was to turn down.

As I passed the gas station, men eyed me and whistled. I was glad that I was wearing my coat, even though from the way they stared I felt as though I was wearing nothing. A car pulled into the gas station and I could see a beautiful woman in a maid's uniform laugh as she caressed the neck of a man who was driving. The man obviously wasn't her husband. As he got out of the car to pump gas, I noticed that he was very well dressed and wore a wedding ring while I hadn't noticed her wearing one as she caressed his neck. I shrugged and continued to walk.

The paved road that I turned down took me downhill. The walk was easier but I knew that coming home would be hard. I only had sandals on. I had brought other shoes with me from home, but they seemed to have disappeared, as did most of the things in my checked bag. I felt my feet begin to throb as I walked down the steep hill and stopped briefly to take a sip of my water. I felt extremely hot, from the sun shining down brightly as it rose in the sky and from the long walk. I could feel sweat rolling down my back as I brushed strands of hair from my face. My face felt dirty and I must have looked twice as bad. I hadn't even looked in the mirror when I woke up since my father was rushing me so much.

Liliana

Not long after I turned down the paved road, I reached the house that my father had spoken of. This wasn't a house I thought to myself as I stopped and stared at it. The house was more of a mansion, being at least several times bigger than my father's. Two guards jumped out at me as I approached the gate. I grasped my chest and lost my breath for a second, my heart skipping a beat out of fright. They had appeared from nowhere and had their guns drawn on me.

"I'm Liliana." I said motioning to my chest, as they questioned me in Spanish.

"I'm here to see Elena." I tried to convince them as they looked at me with cold gazes penetrating my skin.

My heart beat within my chest hard as I fought off the urge to turn around and head home.

"Elena." I said again, louder this time, showing them the uniform that my father had given me.

"Omar, Julio." A woman's voice said from an upstairs balcony. "Dejarla entrar."

I looked up, putting my hand to my face, attempting to shield the sun from my eyes. I could see a woman with wavy dark hair and a long white dress on the balcony. She looked down at me and I could tell from the distance that she was very pretty, but just a little older than me.

"Liliana, I'll be right down." The woman called.

I felt nervous as the guards turned my way and nodded. My body trembled as they opened the gate and motioned for me to go inside with their guns. It appeared they didn't want the gate open for too long, so I rushed inside, looking back to see if anyone else had seen me nearly have a heart attack up walking to the gate. What my father had gotten me into? I looked at the mansion and walked toward it. This was not a house as my father described, it was huge. It was definitely larger than any house I'd ever seen, even in Chicago.

There was a fountain with fish swimming in it, I noticed as I walked by. The grass went on within the gates for what seemed like a mile in either direction. I looked around in shock and wished that my father lived in a place like this. I wondered if his attitude toward me would be different, if he did. I heard the gates slam closed behind me and I turned back to look. The guards were gone. They had disappeared to wherever they were hidden. I took a deep breath and stared at the house. As I looked up at the roof I noticed that there were two more guards stationed on top with binoculars.

"Oh my God." I mumbled to myself, feeling scared to move forward.

I reluctantly walked over to the door and was about to knock, when it was flung open by the woman. She didn't smile as she looked at me. Her eyes seemed to access me as she looked me up and down.

"I'm Elena Chavez-Valencia, daughter of Antonio Salvador Valencia." She said in English quickly, with a noticeable accent.

She didn't look too much older than me I thought, eighteen at the most. Her long wavy hair flowed around her, making her bright face look angelic.

"I'm Liliana Suarez, daughter of Enrique Suarez and Victoria Jacobs." I said, stuttering as I spoke.

She stared at me with a confused expression on her face for a moment.

"You don't know who my father is, do you?" She replied sarcastically.

"No I don't. I'm sorry, I just moved here." I replied, feeling a little nervous.

Her eyes studied me questionably as she stood completely still.

"Should I?" I nervously said as I stared back at her, not knowing what else to day.

She looked slightly taken back. Her eyes told me that she was thinking over my response. Suddenly she looked relieved, as she shook her head and reached up to play with the left side of her hair.

"No it's not important. It's probably better that you don't know him." Elena said, as a smile formed on her face.

I noticed that she had perfect teeth when she did. I couldn't help focusing my attention on them as she spoke. I hoped that she hadn't noticed as she stepped back and invited me in, grabbing my arm in hers, which startled me, but I allowed it as she continued to smile and walk me through the doorway and down a long white hallway. She seemed suddenly overjoyed in meeting me. I could feel her warmth penetrating my arm and I abruptly felt relaxed. Maybe I wouldn't mind working, I thought to myself.

"I live here with my husband and two children, Christina and Nina." She said, turning to me as she led me down the hallway.

"You will be caring for them when they are here. Aside from that, I will need you to do some cleaning." She said quickly. "There will not be too much to do, because the maids do most of the housework."

"Your girls have pretty names." I replied quietly. I thought about what she had just said. *She had two children already?* I noticed a huge diamond ring on her ring finger. Her husband must be older, I thought to myself as I looked around. That must have been the case for her to have all of this. I looked around the room at the lavish decorations and furniture.

"I'm glad that you're so young." Elena suddenly said and I raised my eyebrows at her.

"I mean, you must be right around my age. I'm eighteen." She quickly explained. "The last nanny my father found me looked like she was about to croak. Maybe one day we'll become friends."

I nodded quickly and she let out a nervous laugh.

"Where should I put this on?" I asked, holding up the uniform.

She nodded to a room. I walked into a room that was covered in marble. It looked more like it should be a master bedroom then a single toilet bathroom. There were elegant statues and figurines lining the walls. I was scared I would break something as I tried to balance myself while removing my jogging pants, quickly changing into my uniform, stuffing my clothes into a bag and then washing my face. I felt refreshed as I went out to meet her.

Just as I approached Elena, my stomach let out a huge growl. My face immediately flushed in embarrassment. She looked surprised, and I immediately apologized, muttering something about the toast just before it did it again. I felt like melting right into the floor as her large perfectly shaped eyes focused intently on me. Her eyebrows rose slightly and she pressed her lips together, before losing her composure.

"Are you hungry?" She asked, laughing as she spoke.

I didn't say anything for a moment and then decided to admit that I was. I bit my bottom lip and nodded my head.

"Liliana if you're hungry say something, we're friends now, and you can tell me anything." She assured me. "Don't think so much of me as a boss, okay?" She said, reaching over and grabbing my hand as she led me through what looked like a ballroom.

"Catalina, bring some breakfast to the dining room." She called over her shoulder.

Elena led me into another large room. This one had a huge cherrywood table in the middle of it with cherrywood chairs that were covered in fine silk padding with a design that looked almost like my mother's kimono she always wore as a dressing gown. The walls had pin-striped wallpaper with gold and brown lines. Elena noticed me gawking at the room and smiled.

"My mother's work." She said simply. "She married me off when I was thirteen, so I told her that she better at least go all out on decorating the house."

No sooner did we sit down in the dining room than Catalina, who was a chunky dark-skinned woman, brought in a plate of steaming eggs, bacon, and diced fruits with orange juice. I thanked her immediately. She smiled, her face revealing deep wrinkles around her eyes. Her curly hair had escaped her high ponytail and fell down across her face.

"We knew you'd be hungry." She replied, motioning at a couple of maids standing in the kitchen. She turned and went back into the kitchen, shooing the other maids back with a wave of her hand.

Elena didn't eat with me. She eagerly asked me questions about America, which I answered as I ate bite after bite of the best tasting eggs I had ever had. When I was done eating, I was embarrassed that I ate so fast. Elena must have thought that I had no manners. I quickly picked up a napkin and wiped my face. She asked me what had brought me here and I paused for a moment, trying to figure out how to tell her. I hadn't had to discuss my mother with anyone yet and I wasn't sure that I wanted to. I sighed as I tried to figure out what to do, looking down at my empty plate and then I looked into her eyes and knew that I could trust her. I began to tell her about my mother and lowered my head. She quickly jumped up and came around the table to hug me.

"I'm sorry. I should have known that." She said quietly.

From that point on, I felt very close to Elena. We talked as though we were sisters, whenever I was there. Her daughters were already three and four and attended a private preschool in the mornings, so we would just talk for hours. I revealed to her that I had never had a boyfriend before. She laughed as though I was joking, before realizing that I was serious, as my face turned a deep shade of red. Many of the other girls that she had gone to school with were already married, though she said that she was the first of her friends to tie the knot.

My only other duty at her house would be to mop the floors. The other maids took care of sweeping and everything else. As I began to mop each day, she would follow me around talking about different things, whatever was on her mind at the time. She interested me, because she never ran out of things to talk about. The other maids passed by smiling, all of them significantly older than the two of us. Elena had a lot to talk about.

Her husband Miguel brought her kids home at two in the afternoon each day. I was surprised the first time that I saw him. He was a good looking man, not much older than her which surprised me on account of their obvious fortune. The girls were pretty, too, and both took after Elena. Elena introduced me to Miguel, the first time I saw him, but Miguel obviously did not care to be introduced to me. He did not even look at me and turned his face. Elena rolled her eyes as he left the room.

"He's not very friendly, but he is a favorite of my mother." She rolled her eyes. I wondered what she meant by that.

The girls kept us busy until six o'clock when it was time for me to go each day. I felt so good about being there, that I did not want to leave. Besides this, I was given the food that I ate there each day and, each day the food was delicious, and much better than anything I ever ate at my father's house.

When Miguel came home for dinner on the first night I was there, Elena reluctantly told me that it was time for me to leave. I got the impression that he did not like associating with the servants or something, when he tapped his fingers on the table for her to return.

I shrugged off his behavior as I left the house.

The walk uphill was not as bad as I thought it would be. By the time I made it home it was dark. There were thousands of mosquitos trying to bite my skin and I was scared to death that I would contract malaria. I was glad that I was wearing my jacket although I felt hot and sweaty. The walk seemed much longer than it was because my feet were so tired.

Liliana

Finally, after what seemed like forever, I reached the neighborhood where my father's house was. I thankfully passed through the gates and almost walked right past our house. There were no lights on in the houses and only one street light at the entrance of the neighborhood. I was tired and my feet throbbed in pain from walking, as I started up the stairs, feeling nervous of what he would say to me.

I paused at the doorway, but then found that it was unlocked. No one came to greet me or ask how my day went as I walked in. My father and his family were gathered around the television watching Spanish soap operas. I walked in slowly and quietly hoping that they would ask me something or to join them. My father looked up with an irritated look on his face as I passed them, glancing longingly at him.

"Liliana, go take a shower and go to sleep," he said gruffly. "You have to wake up early tomorrow for work."

I walked into my room and grabbed a towel that was lying on my bed, bending down to look for my pajamas in my duffel bag. Madrigal ran to my room with a sandwich and immediately Teresa scolded her and called her back from the hallway outside of my room. I noticed that my father's wife had on lipstick and some makeup. The look on her face still made her look ugly. I picked up the sandwich that Madrigal had left me and headed to the bathroom.

I ate quickly and got in the shower only to find out that the water didn't get any hotter than lukewarm. Great, I thought to myself. I really wanted to take a long hot shower to relax my exhausted muscles. *Oh well, what did I expect*? I quickly showered, dressed and walked back to my room, stopping to glance down the hallway at my father and his family, before reluctantly going into my room.

I carefully climbed onto my straw bed, thinking about my mother and how the things that she told me about my father were true. My heart felt cold and lost, within my chest. I quickly thanked God for at least letting me have Elena. I really needed a friend to get me through this. I doubted that my father even cared that my mother had died.

As I lay in bed the sounds of gunshots entered my mind with each vision of my mother's face. I pressed my eyes shut to get rid of the sounds but it only worsened. I told myself that I would get over it, but I spent many nights crying for her.

It didn't hurt to think of her as much as the years passed and my time in Colombia began to fly by. It came to the point where my only thoughts consisted of things that I would talk with Elena about the next day.

My days went pretty much the same over the next three years. I would wake up early in the morning and walk to Elena's house each day, feeling very alone when I wasn't with her. She could talk for hours about absolutely nothing and I still found her to be very entertaining. I found out that her mother forced her to get married for her own protection after her brother went away to school in the United States. Her mother had been worried that the guerillas would kidnap her because they tried once before when she was a little girl as a way to make money off of the kidnapping and fund their own political movement.

Miguel was Elena's brother's best friend and her mother arranged the marriage just after he left for college, without his knowledge. Her brother had been pretty upset, especially after she became pregnant with their first daughter and only had come home once to visit in the last eight years. Elena mentioned that he had just graduated from a University with his Master's Degree and that her mom and dad had recently returned from attending the graduation ceremony. Apparently they had smoothed things over, because her brother called Miguel just a week before Elena's daughter's big birthday bash to wish everyone well.

Elena asked her mother several times for pictures of the ceremony, but everything was pushed aside as she struggled to get her daughter's birthday party in order. I was very excited because not only did I get to help plan the party, but for the first time ever, my father was allowing me attend one of the parties that Elena invited me to. I worked for Elena everyday but Sunday, so the party being on a Sunday was a big deal to me. Usually on Sundays, my family would put on their best clothes and go to church, leaving me at home and in charge of cleaning the entire house while they were away. This Sunday my father's *Suegra*, his mother-in-law, was visiting and he wanted me out of the house as much as possible while she was there.

I wasn't complaining. The fact that Elena's party was on a Sunday worked out nicely for me. The only excitement that I had on Sundays was that I had access to the television while they were gone. There were two English shows that I watched on Sundays. One helped the people in Colombia learn English, but in turn, it helped me to learn to understand Spanish better. I would take notes in a small notebook that I had asked Elena for and then go over them during the week while alone in my room at night with the flashlight that I had borrowed from Elena. The other was a show from England that I didn't particularly like, but watched anyway despite its terrible jokes.

My notebook and educational shows were the closest that I had to any form of schooling. My father said that he didn't have the money to put me in what I thought of as a high school, though his other two children did attend elementary school with no problem. My father had enough money to buy them new school uniforms every year, no matter how much he complained about it. He had enough to dress himself well and to buy my stepmother makeup, which was somewhat of a luxury in my opinion. I noticed many of the neighbors giving her dirty looks as they drove off on Sunday mornings.

This Sunday, I was up and ready to go before dawn. I sat waiting on the porch until Elena's limousine pulled onto my street to pick me up. A few of the neighbors were watching me from their doorways as I climbed in. Her bodyguard gave them a stern expression and they quickly turned their heads away. Elena took me to store after store, buying me things to wear for the party. I could feel my excitement grow as I tried different things on for her.

At the last store that Elena took me to, she decided that I would try on dresses for her.

"Liliana, you have Chi-Chi's!" She exclaimed, poking at them as she spoke. I had known Elena since I was fourteen and I'd been somewhat flat chested. I felt my face turn bright red and ran my hands down my sides feeling the silky material of the dress, nervously. My hand brushed against the tag, but I didn't look down. I knew that whatever the price was, I didn't want to see it.

"Do you like it?" I asked. I couldn't remember owning anything this nice even when I was in America. Elena nodded and went on about how much she liked me in blue.

"Turn around and walk for me." She said.

"Wow that really brings out the color of your eyes!" She exclaimed as I walked back toward her. My face felt hotter as I blushed and she pulled me right over to the register to pay for the dress and a pair of high heeled shoes that she had picked out for me, ripping off the tag and handing it to the cashier.

We raced back to her house to make sure that everything had been set up for her party.

It was a beautiful day and the party was going to be outside. Ordinarily this type of party cost a fortune, but Elena's father insisted on having the party for his oldest granddaughter. Elena's father seemed to have connections everywhere so it was costing him next to nothing anyhow from what he told her. Her father was some sort of vigilante in the area, which I didn't understand or ask what it was that he did. To me, he was an extremely intelligent man. He always talked to me when he came around. He often asked me questions about America and where I was from and talked to me about his son that was in school there.

Elena's mother on the other hand was completely different. Her attitude toward me was pretty much the same as Miguel's. When Elena introduced me to her mother, her mom seemed to gaze straight through me. She refused to shake my hand and scolded Elena for associating so closely with the help. Elena tried to explain to her that I was also her friend, but she didn't want to hear it. Elena's mother never hesitated to hand me her jacket when she walked into the house, even if one of the other maids offered to take it. She would also let me know when she was hungry, never looking at me in doing so. She made it my job to call for her food when she visited and never looked at me when she put in her requests.

Elena began introducing me to her relatives as her best friend, instead of as her nanny or as her maid. Elena's mother and father said nothing to blow my cover and for the next four hours I was in heaven as I was allowed to relax and have a little fun.

Although none of her relatives were around our age, a few of the men gave me an admiring look and were extra friendly toward me. One tried to get me to have a shot of Tequila with him, and I politely excused myself and went to sit down with Elena's mother.

I thought that she would be upset that I had invaded her space as she sat snacking on food with her sister, but instead she smiled at me and joked about Elena's big belly. Elena was having her third child soon, her first baby boy. Her husband was ecstatic. She was due any day. Her husband kept coming over to rub Elena's belly and pointed it out to all of his friends that were there with their wives. Miguel had surprisingly even begun talking to me when he found out that Elena was having a boy. Elena was extremely annoyed by the end of the night and looked like she would break down in tears because various family members kept coming over to her and telling her how big she had gotten.

"Stay over." Elena said when I tried to leave. "You're coming back anyway in the morning anyway right?"

I nodded but insisted that I had to leave. I wanted to stay, but I didn't want my welcome to be worn out. Elena's limo driver had already left to take her mother and father home, since their personal driver had requested the night off. I wasn't sure that he would be back anytime soon, so I told her that I would walk. I had thoughtlessly left my jacket at home and was regretting it now as the rain clouds began to appear. I ran for a few blocks, carefully. I was still wearing my high heels, but it was no use. About an hour into my walk the rain had begun to fall and I was quickly drenched.

My new dress was ruined. The blue coloring had started to run down my legs. Mud was now covering the heels of my shoes from the semi dirt road and it was difficult to pull them out as they sunk into the mud. I bent over to take them off, noticing that I had splatters of mud all over my dress. I should have stayed over, I thought to myself. The rain began to fall harder and I could not see where I was going. I stayed close to the side of the road so that I wouldn't get lost.

Suddenly an SUV passed by, headed in the opposite direction and splashed more mud on my new outfit. I screamed out in disgust, looking down at my dress. I looked up just as the SUV stopped and slowly backed up toward me. I stood up straight and tried to look as malicious as possible. The driver side window rolled down a crack.

"Lo siento mucho." A male voice said from inside the truck. I knew that he had said that he was sorry and I quickly nodded, without moving. I was scared of what might happen if I turned my back to the vehicle. I could not see the man through the heavy rain or the tinted windows. The man put his hand through the window with some money.

"Toma esto. Para compensarlo." He said in Spanish. I stood there for a minute without saying anything and shook my head. I turned and started walking, but I couldn't see even a foot in front of me. It had started raining harder.

He beeped his horn. The car reversed slowly toward me.

"Oh God, I'm going to die." I muttered under my breath.

"Vamos. Te voy a dar un paseo." The man said.

He was offering me a ride. I was glad that my Sunday Spanish shows had taught me enough to understand him. I didn't feel comfortable enough answering him in Spanish and debated on running as fast as I could toward my house. I hesitated for a moment and then I thought to myself, what's the worst that could happen? I was getting colder by the second and knew that if I continued to walk, I would be sick the next morning.

"I don't speak Spanish." I said to the man in the SUV through his tinted window. There was a pause for a moment and I wondered if he understood me.

"I said I'm sorry and that I'll give you a ride to make up for it." The voice said, now in perfect English. Now it was my turn to pause. I knew my life couldn't get any worse than it was.

"Come on. I'm not going to hurt you." The voice said convincingly. I told myself that it was a stupid decision, but I decided to get into the car. I ran around the side and opened the door as I jumped up into the high SUV, splashing water onto his dashboard in doing so. I looked at the water beads dripping down his black dashboard and at his rosary that hung from his rear view mirror. I didn't look at him for a moment as I sat there wringing out the bottom of my dress and then noticed that I was getting water all over his carpet.

"I'm sorry." I said to him as I continued to look down in the dark, wiping the wet strands of hair from the sides of my face.

He was quiet. I could feel him staring at me in the dark. I started to get nervous when he didn't start driving right away, but instead he turned on the inside lights of his car. I could feel my heart begin to thump heavily as I sat with my hands folded in my lap, too scared to look over at him. If he was going to hit me with something in my head, I didn't want to see it coming. My mind filled with fear, in imagining what could potentially happen to me. Finally he began to speak and to my surprise, his voice relaxed me.

"Hi, I'm Antonio." He said.

I saw his hand reach out toward me, intending for me to shake it. I wiped my hands on my wet dress and extended my hand as I slowly looked over at him. He took my hand and held it in his for a long moment, smiling. As I stared up at him, I was startled by his eyes. They were dark brown and honestly, the most stunning eyes I had ever seen. He was extremely handsome and there was something about him that made me squeeze my legs together as I became lost in his gaze.

Chapter Six

After three minutes of silence, he awkwardly cleared his throat. I nervously struggled to find something to say but was lost in his looks. His smile made me want to touch it. He had a dimple on one side of his mouth that sunk deeply into his face. I felt like I was melting deeper and deeper into my seat as he held my hand. He was definitely the best looking man I had ever been this close to. I felt my face blush hard as our eyes met. I knew that he was waiting for my answer but I sat admiring him without saying a word. I simply was trying to memorize every detail of this godlike man that sat before me.

I could tell that he was tall, even sitting in the driver's seat. His dark curly hair made me want to run my fingers through it, as the dim car light cast a glow around him. His chin was chiseled and seemed to point down at his shoulders where I couldn't help but admire his muscular build, which popped out from his almost tight tee shirt. I felt my body get weak. I glanced up into his questioning eyes, remembering that he had just introduced himself to me. I grasped the leather seat with my free hand and tried to remember what my name was. I tapped my foot against the floor of the car in anxiety.

"My name is Liliana." I said, pulling my hand away from him quickly and turning my head to look out the window.

I didn't want him to realize that I thought he was the handsomest man that ever walked the earth. I was sure that he could read my expression. I could feel myself blushing and wondered if he had noticed. My heart was pounding so hard that I thought that he could hear it. I tried to keep my composure and pressed my lips together as I debated on whether or not to jump out of the car and run as far away from him as possible as a result of my nervousness.

"Ah, mind if I call you Lily?" He asked.

I could hear the smile in his voice. I turned quickly and looked at him in shock.

"What, did I say something wrong? Do you have a boyfriend?" He asked, grabbing my hand again.

I shook my head and looked down at my hand, which had now gone limp in his grasp. This was it. I was sure that he could tell that I had somehow fallen in love with him in the matter of seconds. Rain pounded on the roof above us and I glanced around before looking him directly in his eyes and becoming lost in his gaze.

"No." I replied slowly, biting my bottom lip. "That's what my mother used to call me and she passed away."

Antonio stroked my limp hand with his thumb. He put his hand to my face and brushed it back against my hair lightly as if he could see the sadness in my eyes. My wet hair stuck to my head as he stroked a few more loose hairs from the side of my face. I studied his every move intently, feeling a tingle from within my breast. I could feel my nipples rising from beneath my dress and was sure that he had noticed them. I tried my best not to look down, so I wouldn't draw any unnecessary attention from him, but saw him glance down as he spoke to me. He bit his lip before beginning to talk.

"Can I take you for coffee, or something?" He asked. "We could talk more."

I thought about it briefly. My father didn't expect me home for at least an hour. I wanted to say yes, but I didn't know who this guy was. What if he didn't take me home or what if he had something up his sleeve? There were not many people that drove this road at night. He had to be a serial killer, I thought to myself.

"I don't think so." I said quickly, somehow regretting saying those words the second they came out of my mouth.

Desire was growing by the second inside me for this man. I felt my panties grow warm and my insides curl up, as he held my hand in anticipation. His eyes looked at me with disappointment, but he did not let my hand go. He stroked it lightly as if to attempt to coax me into saying yes.

"Do you have a curfew?" Antonio asked.

I thought about his question momentarily. My father had not actually told me what time to be home. I felt uncomfortable as I knew my body was taking control and would soon have me saying yes. I shook my head without batting an eyelash. There was something about his eyes that made me feel comfortable.

"No, not really." I replied slowly.

"Well, come on then." Antonio said in a voice that I couldn't resist. "I promise that, I won't bite."

I gazed into his eyes, pushing my foot hard against the floor.

"Alright." I replied as calmly as I could.

A smile was growing across my face and I tried to force it away with the turn of my head. I still felt slightly uncomfortable and yet at the same time, I was glad to be in his presence. I didn't pull my hand away and he didn't let go of it. I glanced out the window but couldn't help turning to look at him every five seconds or so. The hairs on my arms stood up, and for some reason I didn't think that it was because I was cold and wet. He smiled as we drove off. I was sure that he could feel my sexual desire toward him. I wondered if he had noticed my nipples calling out to him, begging him to reach out and stroke them.

As we drove, I felt overcome with thoughts about him. I looked at our hands. Was I supposed to pull my hand away from him? He turned the heater on full blast, so that I could get both dry and warm, and then reached to the seat behind us, letting my hand go, and pulled out a towel.

"Here," he said, glancing over at me.

"I use this when I go running." He said, his lips spreading into a smile again. I pressed my knees together and looked up at him without taking it.

"Don't worry. It's clean." He said, noticing my hesitation.

"I didn't get a chance to use it today." He explained.

I looked over at him and smiled.

"My plane arrived late and I figured I'd go for a jog before checking in with my family." He said. "Then it started pouring rain and I found you instead."

"Thank you." I managed to mutter, as I took the towel and began drying my hair with it.

He glanced over at me as he continued to drive. Our eyes met momentarily and I felt as though I knew him from somewhere. I couldn't get over how handsome he was. I wiped my face with his towel, breathing in his scent, embedded into the fibers. It felt warm against my cold skin. I rubbed my hair and patted my shoulders with it afterward, realizing that I was enjoying the towel too much, when I caught him glancing at me and grinning.

"You're so beautiful." He said to me, smiling and turning to glance at me, while licking his lips.

I smiled and began to blush more heavily. I looked away without turning my head. I couldn't help it, I didn't know what to say. He kept glancing over at me as he drove. His dark eyes seemed to study me and I tried to study him without seeming too interested. I had only known him for a few minutes, but I knew that I was in love with him. I tapped my fingers on the door nervously, searching for the right way to respond. In all of the novellas that I had watched at Elena's house, when two people were attracted to each other, they began kissing and ended up in bed. I definitely wasn't ready to take it that far with him, despite the burning sensation that was growing between my legs as I sat next to him.

"I like your truck." I finally uttered, nervously, immediately questioning myself about what I had just said.

I looked away from him the moment the words left my mouth. I didn't know what to say to a man. I wondered if he could tell how nervous I was. I had never been on a date with a man, let alone held a real conversation with one.

"Do you?" He asked, smiling as he very excitedly told me about the car without waiting for a response.

This was my chance to study him. I had no idea what he was talking about, but I smiled as I watched his lips move. He said something about an engine and horse power, but all that I focused on were his smooth lips. Juicy, I thought to myself. I was ashamed seconds later, for the thoughts that began to go through my mind as I sat listening to him talk about the car being automatic. Were his muscles moving as he was speaking to me, I wondered? I caught myself licking my own lips, as I watched him. I told myself that I needed to focus on what he was saying.

"Do you know how to drive?" He asked.

I shook my head.

"I'll have to teach you." He said quickly as he smiled and looked away.

His smile was contagious, I thought to myself, as my lips spread in to a wide grin.

We passed my neighborhood and entered a part of town that I had never been to. People bustled about the streets, going from stores to restaurants as they happily chatted with each other. I felt sheer happiness flow through my veins as I watched them. For a moment I forgot that I was in a car with a man who I was overwhelmingly attracted to. I hadn't been to a restaurant since I left Chicago, I thought to myself, and grew increasingly excited as Antonio talked about his car.

Antonio stopped the car abruptly after someone dashed across the street without so much as looking back. I glanced over at him, feeling startled. He smiled at me and continued talking. His eyes shined with excitement as he spoke. He began to tell me about the area and about the types of food sold at various restaurants. His voice was soothing. As much as I tried to fight it, my feelings for him grew stronger by the minute.

He unexpectedly made a U-turn and pulled over in front of a fancy restaurant. I noticed a crowd of teenage girls stop to look at Antonio as he walked around the side of the car and handed a valet his keys. The valet driver smiled at him immediately and shook his hand. I felt confused as I watched their expressions. The valet driver looked nervous as he spoke with him. I couldn't quite put my finger on whether or not he was happy to see him. I quickly looked away as Antonio approached the car.

"The food is great here." Antonio said as he opened the door for me and took my hand.

I allowed him to lead me toward the restaurant and couldn't help but smile at the girls as he did so. The looks they gave me made me feel inferior to them. They had on stylish clothing and although Elena had bought my dress at a designer store, it was dirty, damp, and nearly ruined. As we continued to walk, I noticed many people on the street staring at me as I passed. It hadn't rained in this part of town. The ground was dry and they must have wondered why I was walking through the city, drenched with water, as if I had just fallen into a swimming pool. I decided not to let my insecurity get to me. I would enjoy this night, there probably wouldn't be another like this.

As I walked next to him, his cologne intoxicated me. I paused as I inhaled his scent, my body filling with desire as I did so. I tried to make my eyes look as if they were questioning him on where he was taking me. He smiled back at me as he led me on. His hands cupped mine and I couldn't help but notice how wide his fingers were, as he quickly rubbed his thumb over the entirety of my hand.

The restaurant that Antonio chose had a line that stretched out the door, filled with anxious people waiting to be seated. They weren't forgiving as Antonio led me past them. The greeter immediately took us to a booth in the back of the restaurant. I wondered how Antonio had alerted him that we were coming. I smiled, glancing back at the line of people waiting and noticed that a guitarist played soft music as he walked around the room.

I knew my father was good friends with several of the people in the restaurant and began to become worried. If my father found out that I was not at Elena's house, he would kill me. One man in particular starred at me disapprovingly as we passed their table. I knew that he was planning to tell my father something, because of his expression. I would worry about it when my father confronted me, I told myself.

My clothes were still damp from the rain, making me feel uncomfortable as I slid onto the vinyl seat awkwardly. Antonio did not stop smiling at me, which made me wonder if I had any mud left on my face. I blushed and excused myself quickly, hurrying to the women's bathroom. I rubbed soapy water against the mud on my dress and stood under the hand dryer for a couple minutes to air my clothes out. A woman that I remembered walking past when we came into the busy restaurant entered the bathroom, staring at me. She walked over to the mirror to apply makeup. I could tell that she was a lot older than me. I tried to ignore her.

She continued eyeing me and walked out slowly when she was done. I shook my head, fixing my hair quickly and then went back out to join Antonio.

When I approached the table, I noticed that Antonio had ordered all types of food for me to try. He couldn't believe that I hadn't tried many of the foods that he pointed out as I stood looking down at the table. He scooted in close to me as I sat down. I didn't know what to do, and accidently leaned against him, as I shifted my weight nervously. I looked up at him, prepared to apologize, but he looked down at me and smiled, insisting that he feed me with his fork.

He put his arm around me and I froze still in my seat, afraid to move. He laughed as I took a bite of whatever he gave me, telling me what it was and waiting to see my expression. I sipped my drink, wondering what it was. It was sweet and I drank more quickly, while he smiled at me, raising his eyebrows.

"What is it?" I asked, but within seconds of drinking it, I felt warmth rush through me and knew that it must have had alcohol in it. Before long, I was feeling a buzz as I tried to maintain my desire for him. I could tell that he could feel the passion that I was feeling growing as he moved ever closer to me, stroking my arm with his hand as we spoke. When I was done eating he sat his free hand on my thigh and began stroking it, which scared me as I sat awkwardly at his control.

I leaned my hand against his knee, to push his hand away from my thigh, laughing with him as he told me a joke. I enjoyed his laugh more than I enjoyed the joke itself.

He glanced down at his hand that I had moved and then down at my blouse. I nervously laughed and adjusted my dress again, realizing that my nipples were poking out more than I thought possible. I glanced around and suddenly felt like everyone in the restaurant was focused on us. I was really embarrassed. I wondered if anyone could tell that this was my first date.

Antonio didn't seem to notice, or didn't care if he did. He continued asking me questions and hanging on my every word. I told him all about my life in America but tried not to talk about Colombia at all. It seemed like he sensed that, but kept asking me how I liked it here and what it was that I did as I avoided those questions, leaning into him as I felt more comfortable with him.

My head began to feel like it was spinning as I glanced nervously around the room and noticed how beautiful many of the women around us were. Some even walked by the table and tried to catch his eye. He didn't glance at anyone other than me that night, which made me feel special. He began to caress my arm, swirling his fingers in circles, as I spoke to him. I felt nervous, but I didn't try to stop him. His touch felt too good.

He listened to my story and when I was finished, he moved in closer, talking softly into my ear. I couldn't hear what he had said, so I turned my head to question him and he tried to kiss me. I pulled away just as our lips brushed. He sat back as if he were confused. I wanted to die of embarrassment as I felt my face turn bright red. My earlobes began to burn as I asked myself what had just happened.

"I'm sorry." He said. "I couldn't resist." I nodded, not looking at him.

"Are you sure that you're not dating anyone?" He asked. I shook my head slightly and tapped my fingers on the table, biting my lip and looking down at my fork. "You look kind of nervous." He said. "Are you worried that someone will catch you here?"

I shook my head nervously, my hands shaking and my whole body feeling tingly inside. I didn't want to tell him that I had never been on a date before. What if he never wanted to take me out again? He looked like he had dated a million women. I should have kissed him, I thought to myself. I didn't because I was so worried that I would do it wrong. He would never want to see me again, I thought to myself. I was so embarrassed.

My face turned from red to pale in a matter of seconds. I put my hand on his arm, as if to tell him something, but no words came out. He studied my expression, waiting for me to say something. My heart began to beat hard within my chest and I looked away. I could feel everyone in the restaurant staring at us. Antonio noticed me looking around at the other tables nervously. He glared around the room and everyone looked away immediately. He laughed and glanced back at me.

"Come on, I'll take you home." He said.

I nodded and scooted out of the seat as he threw some money on the table. I felt so uncomfortable that I nearly ran out of the restaurant. I could feel eyes from each of the tables beaming in on me. I felt ashamed for pulling away from him. If only I had let him kiss me, everything would have still been fine, I thought to myself. I was in no hurry to get back to my father's house, but the second we were outside of the restaurant, I began to walk even faster. Antonio struggled to keep up with me.

"If you don't want to take me home, it's okay. I can walk from here. It's not that far." I said over my shoulder, even though I didn't have the slightest clue of how to get home from the city. He grabbed my hand and stopped me, motioning for the valet to pull up the car.

"Lily, I want to take you home." He said looking at me with his big brown eyes and smiling gently.

I turned back to stare at him. Tears welled up in the corners of my eyes as my emotions began to go crazy.

We stood quietly staring at each other until the valet brought Antonio his car. Antonio opened the door for me, and I climbed in.

Antonio leaned into the car, putting my seatbelt on for me. He leaned over me in doing so, his hand brushing my thigh. I shivered as I glanced to the side, hoping that he hadn't noticed, though his expression told me that he knew exactly how nervous he was making me.

"Lily you are so fascinating to me. Believe me, I want to see you again. I don't want you to feel uncomfortable around me the next time, though." He said soothingly and I nodded.

"I'd like to see you again, too." I managed to reply. "I'm sorry about back there, it's just that… Well, to be honest, I've never kissed anyone before."

My voice wasn't cooperating with me as I spoke. It crackled as each word was uttered from my mouth. Antonio stared at me and smiled for a long moment, kissing me on the forehead before going around to his side of the car and climbing in, to drive me home.

I gave him directions and told him to stop a block away from my house. My father would kill me if he saw him. Antonio handed me a card with his name and his phone number on it. I glanced down at it in my small hand.

"Call me this weekend." He said. "My number is on there."

I didn't look back down at it, but held it tightly as I smiled at him and then, I got out of the car and walked toward my father's house.

I turned to glance back at him once more as I approached my door. He nodded, but I could feel him watching me to see if I would go in. I saw him drive by my house slowly a minute after I entered the door. I smiled to myself. The house was completely quiet, though I thought that I heard someone wake up as I walked in. I went straight to the shower, spinning around a few times before I got in. When I was done, I went to my room feeling so happy that my bed felt like feathers instead of straw as I sat down on it in the dark.

Not even a minute had passed when Madrigal, now ten years old, appeared at the door.

"You look so happy." She said in perfect English. I looked up at her in surprise.

"I am happy, but when did you learn English?" I asked.

"I have a friend at school who has been teaching me." She replied nervously. I smiled at her as she spoke.

"I know that you are my sister. I wanted to learn English so I could talk to you." She said.

I looked at her in shock. I didn't know how to respond. I nodded at her and she smiled.

I remembered the card Antonio had given me and immediately picked it up, planning to hide it when she left the room. Madrigal glanced to the side and my father came into the room before I could think of anything to say.

Madrigal quickly went back to her room.

I tried to push the card under my pillow, as my father stood watching me without saying a word. He saw it as I did and took it from me, crumbling it in his hand. A tear of fear rolled down the side of my face as he stared at me intently, his face full of fury.

He pulled off his belt in all of two seconds, giving me little time to prepare for what was coming. I shuddered and he whipped me right on the shoulder, narrowly missing my face.

"Why were you talking to her?" He yelled. "What did you tell her?"

"Ow!" I cried out in pain. Teresa woke up and went to the kitchen.

"I didn't say anything!" I screamed, touching my shoulder as it stung with pain. He swung the belt again, this time hitting my back as I turned away. My back arched when the belt made a sharp connection with my wet skin.

"Why do your clothes smell like men's cologne?" He yelled, gritting his teeth as he spoke.

"I don't know." I cried out. "There were a lot of men at Elena's party."

He hit me again with the belt in the same place on my back and I screamed as I felt blood dripping from my skin.

"You cheap whore!" He yelled, pulling me from the bed by my hair.

I fell on the floor and cried in pain.

"Stop it! You're hurting me!" I screamed as he hit me again. This only encouraged him and he began to kick me repeatedly behind my thighs.

"Estás tratando de matar a la chica?" I heard his wife Teresa whisper loudly from the doorway, her arms crossed against her chest.

My father stopped immediately. I could feel his wife's pity as she glanced at me before walking away. My entire body burned in pain as I lay in a ball on the floor. He glared angrily at me for a minute as I tried to get up, my legs feeling the pain of his beating before any other part of my body. He walked away, taking the crumbled card with him and ripping it up as he walked.

I managed to pull myself onto my bed after two or three minutes, aching from head to toe.

I tried to pretend I didn't feel the burn from the belt on my skin or the pain in my body, as I lay still upon my bed.

"Dear Lord." I prayed. "Please help me. I'll do anything to get away from here." I said softly while I wondered why my life was so miserable.

"Give me a sign." I said again softly and began to think of my mother. I wished that my mom had never died and that I had never come here. I was in such pain that I didn't even think about Antonio and the great time that we'd had. My only thoughts were of how evil my father was and the cruel way that he treated me.

The next morning when I woke up the skin on my back and shoulders burned. I didn't want to move. I lay in bed as long as possible, even though I knew that I had to be at Elena's house soon. I weighed my options as I removed my pajamas, the material sticking to the wounds. I thought back to the night before and smiled, as the memory of Antonio again came into focus. It had definitely been worth it, I thought. I knew that I was in love with him. I remembered the card and became sad. How would I ever see him again?

I couldn't wait to tell Elena about him and to ask for her opinion. Maybe she would be able to help me find him. It was really hard to even get dressed, each part of my body stinging in pain each time I bent or put my clothes on, against my bruised and cut skin. I felt like absolute crap as I walked slowly out of my room, holding my jacket in my hands.

My father stood nearby waiting for me and grabbed me by the arm.

"Where are you going?" He asked.

"To work." I said halfheartedly.

"I'll drive you to make sure that's where you're really going." He said. His wife stood beside him watching him, as if to make sure that he didn't hit me again.

"Fine." I replied coldly. I hadn't wanted to walk this morning anyway.

We climbed into his car, him in the driver's seat and me in the backseat. I hadn't been in his car since the day he picked me up at the airport. That was over three years ago. I couldn't believe that now after all this time he decided to drive me to work. His seats were plush and felt cushy. I glared at my father in hatred as he turned on his radio. I didn't dare speak to him. He had a look in his eyes that scared me.

We sat in silence. I grew very tired from staring out the window at the shrubbery alongside the road. I tried to keep my eyes open, but the silence and heat made me get drowsy as I laid my head against the window and closed my eyes. When I woke up I was alone in his car, parked in the middle of the town square. There were merchants setting up their booths up and down the block. I glanced around nervously as sweat dripped down my face from the heat. I haven't been here before, I thought. I wondered where he had taken me.

My father suddenly walked up to the car with a younger man who looked dirty. His clothes did not match and he looked like he was on drugs as he tried to balance himself. There was a woman standing on a corner nearby watching and shaking her head. She wore a mini skirt, heels and a tank top, with no bra. She must be with the man, I thought. The man looked down at me in disgust. I sunk down in my seat, pulling my coat up and over my chest, where the man had his attention directed. The man raised his eyebrows and turned away, glancing over to the woman, who waved her finger at him. My father nodded at me.

"Que crees?" He asked the man. The man shook his head.

"Nah, es muy weda." The man turned to leave, walking back over to the woman and slapping her butt. The two then started laughing as two more women dressed the same way walked over to them, glancing at our car as the man spoke to them. I knew what the man had just said. He said I was too light-skinned. My father threw his hands up as I sat in shock. He got inside the car, slamming the door and began tossing things around before he put his keys in the ignition and started the car.

"Were you trying to sell me?" I asked my father. He just smirked and drove off to Elena's.

"I might as well try to make some money off of you before you're not worth anything." He said. "Let me find out that you do this again and I will let the guy keep you, if you want to act like a slut, coming home smelling like his cologne."

"I am not a slut." I yelled. I was too mad to say anything else. Tears formed in the corners of my eyes and I crossed my arms. I couldn't believe my own father had said this to me.

As he approached Elena's house, he turned back to look at me. His pupils were dilated and he looked scary as he began to speak. "You come straight home. Don't let me hear about you going on a date again. Do you understand?"

I nodded my head and thought over whether I wanted to go back home or not. What if he was successful the next time he tried to leave me on some street corner? I wished that I had somewhere else to stay. I could not take the chance that what happened this morning would happen again. I had come to hate him with such a passion. I couldn't understand how he thought the way that he did.

I walked past the guards, noticing that there were several cars in the driveway. This wasn't unusual. Sometimes Miguel would host meetings at his house for their family members. When I walked in the door, everything was quiet. This was not normal, I thought as I glanced nervously around. I saw one of the maids folding clothes in another room. She looked up and smiled at me.

"Elena," I called, but there was no response. The maid put her fingers to her lips, as if to tell me to be quiet and I assumed that Elena was sleeping. I didn't think anything of it and went to get the mop out of the closet. I stood in the mop closet putting my hair into a ponytail, and I thought about what I was going to tell Elena. I would get my work done early, I thought. She was probably sleeping and maybe Catalina was out doing errands.

I clenched my teeth down in pain as I bent over to turn the water on. I felt the tension growing inside of me as I thought about my father and Antonio. As I stood in the closet preparing the mop bucket, the dining room doors opened. I looked up to see Elena's father, followed by a few relatives that I didn't know come out. I started to come out to greet them, but then Elena walked out with her mother and of all people, Antonio. I tried not to gasp as I ducked deep into the closet, but the closet was at an angle, where they could see straight in, and unless I clung to the wall, they would see me.

Elena glanced over at the closet and saw me, but everyone else stood talking with one another. She pressed her lips together as I watched her expression, shaking my head nervously through the opening of the closet door.

"Liliana, come here." Elena called out. "Let me introduce you to my brother."

My heart felt like it cracked in half at that moment. I gulped down what seemed to be like my entire tongue. Everything suddenly made sense to me. Antonio was her brother. Despite the fact that I must have looked thoroughly confused and had nearly swallowed my own tongue, I stepped out of the closet slowly. I hoped that he didn't recognize me with my hair pulled back.

"Hi," I forced myself to say lightly as I looked down for a moment, before looking up to see his expression.

Antonio looked as surprised as I felt. He did recognize me, I could tell. I knew he wouldn't want to see me again, now for sure. I wondered if my day could possibly get any worse. The two of us stood there examining each other's expressions for what felt like forever. His father and several of his uncles looked at each other, raising their eyebrows at one another and nodding. Did they know, I wondered?

"This is Liliana, my best friend and my nanny." Elena broke the silence as she smiled. She looked from me to her brother as she studied the expressions that we gave each other. Antonio remained silent as he stared at me. He had a look on his face that made me wonder what he was thinking. Perhaps he didn't like associating with the help, the same way Elena's mother and husband didn't. My heart sank. I felt as though it had stopped beating. I thought over backing into the closet and closing the door.

"Liliana, this is my brother Antonio." Elena said, looking over at him, giving him a strange expression as she waited for him to say something.

His eyes seemed to light up, after hearing his name. Antonio smiled, staring at me directly as he put his hand out.

"Pleasure to meet you, Lily," he said. His beautiful smile suddenly appeared on his juicy lips.

I smiled. I took his hand and shook it trying to make it look like it was the first time we had ever met. Antonio's hand shake was firm. My hand seemed to melt inside of his. He did not let go of my hand right away and I was scared that someone may have noticed. I tried to pull my hand away, but he raised my hand to his mouth and kissed it, not taking his eyes off of me the entire time. His mother, though standing across the room, eyed both of us closely. I felt my knees go weak and I pulled my hand away. I hoped no one had noticed the goose bumps that had popped up on my skin, or knew how I must be feeling at this exact moment. It was hard to hide my feelings with my face turning bright red.

I smiled nervously as I looked around the room at everyone watching us. No one was moving. They were just taking the moment in along with us. I stepped back, picked up the mop and immediately turned in the opposite direction, setting off to mop down the hallway, as far away as I could get from all of them. I had to get out of there, I thought to myself. Elena's father smiled as I walked past, while Blanca stood staring at me in disgust.

"Well, we better get going." Antonio Salvador said. "The meeting is at twelve and we still have to take your mother home."

Antonio nodded and then gave Elena a hug, saying goodbye to the other relatives as he left with his parents.

Chapter Seven

I felt like I was walking on air after seeing Antonio again. I thought of the conversation that we had the night before as I mopped the floor. I remembered how he sat in the car as I walked toward my house and wondered why he had watched me go, when I noticed Elena staring intently at me from across the room. She leaned against the wall as she watched me and smiled when I noticed her. Elena was my best friend, I thought to myself. How could I even think about dating her brother? Elena lifted her hands to me, as if to question me. All that I could do was smile at her as my mind went crazy with thoughts of Antonio. I wanted to come clean with her, but what would she think? What if he didn't want to be with me after seeing me in my maid's uniform? It was obvious that his mother noticed something and I already knew how she felt about me.

Elena walked toward the stairs, motioning for me to follow her. I reluctantly trailed behind her. I knew what was coming and became nervous as she led me to her room and closed the door.

She looked excited, like she knew the biggest secret in the world. She glanced out the window and then went to sit on the bed.

"Come on. Have a seat." She said motioning to her bed. I slowly walked across the room and sat down next to her.

"So my brother came back from the United States yesterday." She said. "Do you find him attractive?"

I paused for a moment and then nodded at her, my face going pale. I wanted to tell her about last night, but I had no idea how to start off. She smiled and folded her hands neatly on her lap.

"Yesterday, when Antonio arrived, he meant to surprise me at the party." She said with a smile on her face, pausing to study my reaction.

"His plane was delayed and of course he didn't make it until much later." She finished off, pausing again hoping that I would say something. I couldn't tell her yet. I was too shy to blurt out my feelings about him.

"When he did arrive, he and I sat and talked for hours and he told me that part of the reason that he was late was that he met someone and took her to dinner." Elena said slowly as I began to blush.

I slowly smiled at her. I could feel my ears burn. She had to know. I wanted to rattle right off and tell her, but something inside me wanted me to wait and hear what else he had told her about me.

"He told me that her name was Lily." She said slowly, waiting for me to say something.

I nodded again, trying hard to control my smile. She smirked at me, as it came obvious to her that I was not going to spill the beans, on this one.

"Today, stupid me, I put two and two together." She said quickly. "I know that it's you that he was talking about. Correct me if I'm wrong, please."

I shook my head.

"Oh." She exclaimed and hugged me. "I never thought this would happen, I don't know why I didn't think to introduce you guys myself. He finished his degree and now he's back for good. This is perfect."

"Elena," I said tensely. "You know I've never had a boyfriend before. I felt like I melted yesterday when we met. I felt so stupid getting into the car with him, but it was pouring rain and I just wanted to go home." I said, taking a deep breath and trying to remain as calm as possible. "I was so scared." I said. "Then... well, I think I'm in love."

She smiled at me, still holding my hand. Her eyes stared deep into my own as though she was attempting to read my mind.

"Liliana, I honestly have never felt like that." She said. "You are so lucky. God, if I could have only felt that type of love, that type you feel from your heart and soul." She looked at me dreamily.

"Would you be alright with it, if maybe I called him?" I asked. "I mean I don't even know if he'll still be interested in me, but you wouldn't mind if I did?"

Elena looked at me with puzzled eyes. She held her hands together tightly as her eyelashes fluttered around. "Of course not, but what do you mean if he'd still be interested in you?" She asked, pausing as she spoke. "Of course he will be. You are beautiful and you're such a sweetheart. I don't know where I'd even be without you these last three years." She sighed, as she spoke convincingly to me. I looked down at my hands. Then I looked at her and around the room.

"Elena, I'm a nanny." I said. "I'm nothing. Look at how your mother looks at me. I can't imagine him wanting to be with me after he saw me this morning." I said sadly. Elena hugged me tightly and kissed my cheek.

"Liliana, Antonio is nothing like my mother." She answered. "You'll see."

She went on to tell me more than she ever had about him. I told her all about what my father had done also. I showed her some of the marks from the belt, embedded into my skin. Her eyes were full of shock. She was upset and told me that if anything like that ever happened again, to run away as fast as I could and call her. We said goodbye to each other and I mopped the floors vigorously when she had to leave for her doctor's appointment. Miguel was meeting her with the girls, so I was on my own for the rest of the afternoon.

When I was finished I looked up at the clock to see that it was already six o'clock. I rushed out so that I would be able to make it home before dark, asking Catalina to tell Elena that I said good-bye as I left. She nodded and went on to prepare dinner.

Liliana

I decided that I would jog home to make sure that my father didn't have anything to complain about. I imagined my father was already waiting with the belt. It was breezy enough that I knew I wouldn't get tired too quickly.

About a mile down the road I heard a horn honk twice behind me. I quickly glanced back and saw a blue car approaching. I looked back at the road in front of me and continued jogging. The car pulled up alongside of me.

"What are you running from?" A male voice asked. "Not me, I hope." I stopped and turned to see Antonio.

"Not from you." I smiled broadly. "I didn't recognize your car."

"I have two more, so be on the lookout." He said, letting out a laugh. "Will you do me the honor of letting me drive you home?"

"Sure." I said jumping in his car without hesitation.

"Mind if we stop somewhere first?" He asked.

"Oh, I can't. My father will kill me." I shook my head as I looked deep into his penetrating eyes.

"I'll take care of your father." He said, scrunching up his nose and giving me a funny look. "Come on, how often do you get to have fun?"

"Me? Never," I replied.

"You see." He said, turning the car around. "Trust me on this."

We both smiled at each other as he reached over and took my hand in his. I glanced down at my hand in his, suddenly feeling very warm inside. We drove for what felt like hours. I pushed any thoughts of my father out of my mind as I noticed the time.

He finally pulled in to a secluded area overlooking the river. He pulled the car right up to the side of the cliff and I could see the water crashing against its base. The view was amazing and scary at the same time. After we got out of the car, I tried to stay as close to the car as possible. Antonio opened the trunk and pulled out a picnic basket and a blanket.

"Ever see the sun go down?" He asked.

I shook my head nervously. I wanted to tell him that I couldn't stay, but I decided that I didn't care what happened with my father. I never had the opportunity to enjoy myself. I was seventeen, nearly eighteen years old and I had spent the last three and a half years of my life completely miserable. I smiled as Antonio laid out the blanket and we sat down. He pulled out two sets of wine glasses, a bottle of wine, silverware, fancy plates, and food that was still steaming hot. I laughed as I glanced over at him.

"Oh my God Antonio! You shouldn't have gone to all this trouble." I said happily, fighting to keep a huge smile from forming on my face.

"It's no trouble." Antonio quickly replied. "It's not often that I meet a nice girl."

I beamed at him.

"Besides, Catalina cooked the food and came up with the idea for me, after I told her that it was you that I met last night."

"Catalina did?" I asked. I felt a glow come to my face. I wondered who else he had talked about me to. He nodded at me and poured me a glass of wine and I looked at it for a minute and could feel myself turning pale.

"What's wrong?" Antonio asked. "The wine was my idea. I picked it up on the way."

"I've never drank wine before." I said.

He shook his head and smiled. "You're kidding me."

I shook my head.

"No wonder you were acting odd with that Margarita the other night."

"Is that what it was?" I asked. He began to laugh.

"I forgot." Antonio said. "Elena told me you were almost eighteen. Well, there's always a first, right?" He asked and laughed, handing me the drink. He must have noticed the scared look on my face as he examined my expression.

"Don't worry Lily. I'll take care of you." He said, rubbing my hand reassuringly. I took a tiny sip and noted that the wine tasted very sweet, almost like grape juice. I gave in and drank it along with my food. We laughed and talked about our lives, eating small bits of the picnic food when we had a moment between.

He poured me more wine each time I started to talk and within about twenty minutes I began to feel dizzy and leaned over to put my head on his shoulder. He smelled so good and I felt as if I were in heaven. He leaned over and kissed my lips lightly. He pulled back to look at my expression and then he did it again, this time slipping his tongue in and moving it around. I did the same and we pulled away, both smiling as we lay on the blanket watching the sun. He had a satisfied look on his face, while I blushed heavily, laying my hand over his chest in an attempt to stop the spinning feeling.

"See, how many guys have taken you to see the sunset?" He asked, holding my hand in his and kissing it. I smiled.

"No guy has actually ever taken me anywhere." I said. "I've never had a boyfriend."

Antonio smiled at me and licked his lips. "Are you serious?" He asked. I nodded. He leaned over and kissed me softly on the lips. "You mean to tell me that no one has ever felt those soft lips on theirs?"

I shook my head, suddenly feeling relaxed and hot all over. He leaned in and kissed me again, this time passionately. I followed his lead as I felt myself inhale heavily and my buttocks tighten. His hand went to my breast and he cupped it and rubbed his fingertip over my nipple until it rose to his touch. I felt both nervous and uncomfortable as he reached around and grabbed my butt to pull me closer to him. I was so close to him that I could feel his manhood grow and I pushed him away as my body began to tingle. I buried my head into his shoulder and sighed, trying hard to fight the overwhelming desire I felt for him.

He looked disappointed, but held my hand as we watched the sun go down. When it was nearly out of sight, he began to talk more about us. I smiled at him and reached up to caress his neck as he spoke. I loved looking at him. When he began to talk about marriage, I knew that this was a face I would enjoy waking up next to each day. Sure we had only known each other for two days, but I knew how I felt about him. I knew no one else would understand and asked him what his mother would think.

"Honestly Lily, I don't care what she thinks." He replied and smiled at me, caressing my arm as we lay there.

I smiled at him, enjoying every second of his touch.

Just when it looked like the sun had gone beneath the water he leaned over to kiss me again, this time pressing down on my shoulder with his hand. I jumped away in pain before our lips had even touched.

"What's wrong?" He asked. "Lily, I'll take care of you. Don't worry. I'm not going to push you to do anything you don't want to do. I just want to kiss you, okay?" He asked.

Tears gathered in my eyes, but I nodded. I didn't want to tell him about my father. I felt like garbage because of the way my father treated me. Antonio kissed me again, touching my shoulder in the same spot, making me jump back again in pain. He pulled back and looked at me dumbfounded.

"No, it's not that, Antonio." I immediately said. "I trust you." I said quietly as I looked down. "My back," I started to say. Tears dropped from my eyes and my lip quivered as I tried to tell him but couldn't. He looked at me in confusion.

"What's wrong, Lily?" He asked. Antonio leaned into me and put his arm around my shoulders to comfort me. His touch was too much for my wounds and I jumped again this time obviously in pain. Antonio noticed and began to look upset. "Are you going to tell me what's wrong?"

I shook my head, as if to say that I couldn't, covering my face with my trembling hands in embarrassment.

"Unzip your outfit." He ordered me. I reached back and unzipped the back slowly and Antonio pulled the sides of the uniform down to reveal my naked back to him. He knelt down beside me and ran his hand delicately over my shoulders and my back, obviously noticing the marks from where my father had hit me. He bit his lip and zipped my dress back up.

He moved and sat directly in front of me holding my hands.

"Who did this to you?" He asked.

I shook my head, trying not to look him in the eye. I didn't say anything and he asked me again more forcefully.

"My father," I finally said, my lip trembling. "He was upset that I came home late yesterday."

Antonio sat back. I could see the anger in his face building as he looked at me. I told him how my father beat me and how he took me to see that man in the morning and about how scared I was. I was hoping that he would give me some kind of response when I finished, but he just shook his head.

"Come on, let's take you home. It's already late." He finally said, kissing me on the top of my head. I didn't want to go home, but I didn't tell him. Was he just listening to my story? He had to know. He motioned to the car as he quickly folded the blanket, not even removing anything from it, just lifting the sides and rolling it in a bundle and tossing it in the trunk.

"Please don't tell him what I told you." I said in a loud whisper as I got in the car.

Antonio glared at me angrily without saying anything. He bit down on his lip and turned the radio on. I gazed out of the window in fear. I knew my father was going to beat me again, but it was worth it, even if I never saw Antonio again. I couldn't tell from his expression what he was thinking.

He drove without saying anything for at least twenty minutes. When he finally began to speak, I felt relief flood my body. "Believe me, I have so much to say to you, Lily." He said. "I don't want you to think I'm not interested in you. I just don't understand your father and how he could treat you this way."

Antonio pulled up at the same spot he had dropped me off at the night before. I glanced at the house and then I turned to look at him as he grabbed my left hand.

"Lily, I think I'm in love with you." He blurted out. My knees shook hard out of fear.

"I can see us together. What do you think?" He asked.

"I'm sure I'm in love with you." I said. "You may be the first man I ever kissed, but I know that I love you." I smiled nervously at him.

He took my face in his hands and kissed me, harder and longer then the last time, as if to see if what I had said was true. I put my arms around his neck and ran my fingers through his curly hair. Our kiss was long and passionate, making me feel hot inside. I became nervous that someone would see us and pulled away reluctantly as I stared at him.

"Thank you for another wonderful night." I said. "Tomorrow, you know where to find me."

I smiled at him naughtily as I opened the door and hesitantly got out. Mosquitos began to bite me as I walked quickly toward my house. I had hardly put my hand on the doorknob when my father flung it open and hit me in the head so hard that I fell inside to the floor. My ankle hit the floor hard and I had a horrible pain shoot through my ankle and up my leg. He kicked me in the side of my stomach and shut the door. Everything happened so quickly, that I forgot Antonio was outside. My father's wife looked up as she sat on the sofa, watching as my father dragged me to my room.

Madrigal yelled out to him to stop as she began to cry hysterically. A second later there was a knock at the door. My father slammed my face into my mattress so hard that the straw broke through the pillowcase and scratched my face. His wife scolded him as he passed her and he swore at her as he continued on to open the door. I heard a thump when he did, followed by a scream from Madrigal.

"I will never allow you the chance to hit Lily again." I heard Antonio shout at my father. "You are lucky that I don't kill you, out of respect for her and for the fact that you are the only parent that she has." Antonio continued. "Consider yourself a dead man if I ever hear of you touching any woman like that again."

I smiled though I couldn't move, my ankle was throbbing in inexplicable pain.

"Llévame a tu hermana." Antonio said. Madrigal appeared in my room a moment later, followed by Antonio.

"Lily, are you ok?" Antonio asked, rushing over to my side. I looked up at him, without saying a word. I tried opening my mouth to speak but the scratches from the straw were deep and made my face sting when I tried to talk. He put his hand over my lips as if to silence me. He could see the pain I was in as he stood still, thinking over what to do.

"Can you put her things in a bag for me, please?" He asked Madrigal. Madrigal stepped over to my bed and kneeled down to pull my suitcase out from under the bed.

"She never really unpacked." Madrigal said timidly, backing away from him and slowly leaving my room.

"Is this everything?" Antonio asked. I nodded.

He lifted me to a standing position as I tried to balance myself on my bad leg. I clung onto him as I walked, my ankle throbbing with pain. As we passed my father, hunched over on the floor with a bag of ice pressed to his eye, my father looked up at us.

"Where are you taking her? You know she is still working off my debt to your family." My father said. "If you want her, I think that you should pay me."

"Consider all debt paid off as of this day." Antonio quickly replied. "Keep this in mind, old man, you are lucky to be alive."

"Give me money for her or I will go to city and let them know that you are back." My father snarled through his teeth.

"Oh, believe me," Antonio replied. "Everyone knows that I am back." Antonio began to walk, before turning to him and gritting his teeth. "Your debt is gone, but that isn't good enough, huh?" He glanced back at me as if he had just remembered that I was there.

My father stared at Antonio with fear in his eyes as he began to speak slowly. "No, it's not." My father said. "What about the food and the home to stay in?" He looked away and then began speaking louder. "Five hundred American dollars or leave the girl."

Antonio laughed. My father joined in and then quickly stopped himself as a sly expression replaced his smile.

"She doesn't need to know who they are does she?" My father asked as he let out a laugh. "Un pensamiento para ti, Antonio." He paused. "She doesn't know who you are either, does she?"

Antonio looked back at me as if my father had just won.

My father smiled, removing the ice bag from his eye. Antonio and my father glared at each other for a few moments. Regardless of my father apparently having the upper hand, Antonio obviously scared my father enough to keep him in his place.

Antonio let go of me a few moments later and reached into his back pocket. He pulled a roll of money held together by a money clip and threw it at my father. Teresa quickly picked it up and began to count it, as my father's instructed.

"I assure you that your daughter is worth far more than five hundred dollars." Antonio said as he turned to walk away, taking my arm and pulling me along as he did. I had no idea what it was that my father knew about Antonio, but I didn't care.

Liliana

Antonio looked back at the house as we stepped out the front door before picking me up and putting me into his car. "Lily, I couldn't leave you." He said as he leaned over me. "You don't feel that I am trying control you, do you?" He asked me. I shook my head. He kissed me softly on the lips before pulling away. We saw Madrigal running toward us.

"Liliana, don't forget me." She said. "Call my best friend Lupe's house, here is her number.

"Madrigal, get in the house now." My father screamed from the doorway. Madrigal turned to him and then paused, looking back at us.

"He's cute." She said. "I hope you guys get married." She then turned around, running back into the house. Antonio smiled as she left.

"Hey, maybe that's a good idea." He called after her. She turned around and waved at us as Antonio drove off into the night. I closed my eyes knowing that when I woke up my problems would be over.

Chapter Eight

Antonio took me to the hospital to get my ankle and wounds taken care of. When the doctor came in, Antonio muttered something to him and they both left the room. Moments later a female doctor came in. The doctor had me get undressed and gave me a thorough exam which I thought was odd, considering Antonio had just explained to the male doctor that my ankle was the problem.

"No, it's my ankle that's hurting." I said to the doctor as she tried to reach inside of me.

"Dear, you haven't had a thorough exam in your life." She replied. "We just need to make sure everything is alright."

I lay back on the table reluctantly, shaking as she checked my insides. When she was done, I quickly put my clothes on and the doctor wrapped my ankle in a cloth bandage. Antonio came back into the room as she finished and I noticed the doctor nod to Antonio. He smiled and paid the doctor in cash from his jacket pocket, making it obvious that he couldn't take his eyes off of me.

"What, do I look horrible?" I asked shyly.

He shook his head. "You're just so beautiful. Your eyes, your nose, your lips, we are going to have the most beautiful children." He said, leaning over as we left the doctor's office. He kissed me softly on my cheek. I blushed as we got back in his car and drove to Elena's.

Miguel opened the door and warmly greeted Antonio. He looked at me and smiled.

"I'll show you to your room." Miguel said. "Elena's sleeping and we know how hard it is for her to fall asleep this far into the pregnancy."

Antonio walked upstairs with us. The room they gave me was about the size of my father's entire house. I was familiar with the room since I'd cleaned its floor, many times, while working for Elena. Antonio entered the room to put my suitcase next to the dresser, quickly stepping out with Miguel.

"You better get some rest." Antonio said as he closed the door and blew me a kiss.

I heard their muffled voices outside my doorway as they walked down the hallway, but could not make out what they were saying. I turned off the light, hobbled over to the bed and smiled as I climbed in. The bed was so soft that I stretched my arms and legs out and let my body sink in. While I had only known Antonio for two days, I was happy that he had rescued me from my father's care. At this point, that was all that I was thinking about and grateful for.

"No way!" I suddenly heard Miguel shout out from the hallway and then laugh loudly. Antonio hushed him quickly and the two of them both laughed as I heard their footsteps going downstairs. Had Antonio told him about what happened with my father, I wondered? Everyone was bound to find out. I glanced at the wall and noticed there was a picture of Antonio hanging on it. I wondered if it had always been there and wondered why I had never noticed it before. I grew tired as I stared at it, falling into a deep sleep immediately.

Chapter Nine

In the morning, the daylight woke me up. I hadn't been able to lie in bed and watch the sun rise since I was younger. This simple act of nature was something that I now learned to appreciate. I watched the sun slowly rise further and further into the sky before sitting up in my bed. Realizing that I had my own bathroom, I quickly undressed and went to shower. As I began to run the water and realized that I had hot water, I felt as though I had died and gone to heaven. I put the plug in and let the water fill to the top of the bathtub, the luxurious bathtub, before getting in.

The hot water felt so good. My skin was sweating from the steam that rose from the water. I leaned my head back against the tub and allowed my body to feel every inch of goodness. The burning sensation relaxed my muscles and helped my ankle to feel better, though at first my skin burned. I felt completely relaxed for the first time in years.

There was a light knock at the bathroom door. I covered my chest as Elena peaked in.

"It's just me," Elena said. "Can I come in?"

I nodded and she entered, going to sit in a chair that was placed near the edge of the tub.

"Antonio was over for breakfast and told me everything." Elena said. "I don't know what to say. I mean I'm sorry for what happened with your father, but I'm glad you're here." She smiled at me.

"How do you feel about my brother?" She asked. "Are you sure that you love him?"

I nodded.

"Has he told you anything about our family or our business interactions?" She asked slowly, glancing at me to study my expression. I shook my head. She looked disappointed.

"Is Antonio still here?" I asked. Elena shook her head.

"No, he only stayed for breakfast and then left with my father." Elena responded. "This is what I mean Liliana, are you going to be okay with him going to meetings every day, leaving you home by yourself?" I nodded.

"I'm in love with him Elena, and right now, that is the only thing that matters to me." I said. "Besides that, I had to get out of my father's house Elena. This worked out perfectly, don't you see?"

"Yes, but being the person my father is means a lot to him." Elena replied. "Now that Antonio's here, he has to learn the business. I'm worried about you and how you are going to feel, having to deal with the type of person that he is going to become."

"What type of business is your family in?" I asked slowly, questioning myself and if I cared about the answer or not. Elena's face turned cold, showing that she was not prepared for me to ask her the question.

"I'm sure Antonio would rather explain it to you." Elena responded firmly.

Her response surprised me.

Elena noticed that she had been snippy with me and quickly tried to make up for it. "I brought you some of my clothes. I can't fit into them anymore, come take a look." She said lightly as she handed me a fuzzy brown towel and then left the room.

I dried off a bit before putting on the towel and going back into my room to meet her.

The bed was covered with clothes on hangers. "Oh my goodness Elena!" I exclaimed. "Is all of this for me? What are you going to wear after you have the baby?"

"Oh, don't worry." She responded. "I already told Miguel that after this baby he's buying me a whole new wardrobe." She laughed out loud.

"I doubt I'll fit back into that stuff at all anyway, most of it is from before I even had Christina." She said.

I immediately grabbed a khaki-colored cotton dress and put it on.

"You look so good in that." Elena said. "Can I do your hair and make-up?" She asked.

I nodded and she began to fix my hair. I got the chills as Elena gently combed my hair, before putting it in a French braid. She used make up to cover all of the scratches on my face. When she finished and I looked into the mirror, I didn't even recognize myself.

"Wow." I said out loud. Elena laughed.

"You look like a model." She said. "My brother hasn't the slightest clue what a gem he found himself." She looked at me, her face beaming proudly.

We went down the stairs slowly and Catalina gave me a surprised look as we entered the room. "Who's this lovely lady?" She asked Elena. Catalina dashed to the kitchen and quickly returned, bringing us our plates, smiling at me the entire time. I giggled.

"Thank you Catalina." I said as she set the plate before me on the table. We ate our food, discussing what happened the night before as Catalina sat down with us. Less than two hours later, Elena went into labor and we quickly rushed her to the hospital. We stood at Elena's side as she gave birth to her son.

Miguel tried his best to get there, but didn't make it until after the baby was born. When we walked out of the delivery area, Elena's entire family was there waiting to hear the good news.

"It's definitely a boy!" Catalina exclaimed. Cheers filled the room.

"He looks like his papa." I heard Catalina say to Antonio Salvador and Blanca. Antonio jumped out of his chair and walked over to me, letting out a whistle.

"Check out my princess." He said boldly, smiling as he took my hand in his. I blushed as he kissed me on my cheek. "You look beautiful."

His family's attention shifted to us, but no one said a word. I felt Blanca's disapproving glare on me. A heavyset man came over to us.

"Antonio, this is the one?" He asked, smiling at me.

"Yes, this is the woman I'm going to marry." Antonio responded. Blanca quickly got up and left the room.

"Liliana, I would like to introduce you to my Uncle Marcus, Colombia's main man." Antonio said to me.

I smiled and shook his uncle's hand. I saw the crinkling in the corners of his eyes and decided that his smile was genuine. A very pretty, middle-aged woman walked over to his side. She wore an orange scarf loosely around her neck and a large pair of matching earrings.

"This is my uncle's beautiful wife, Roberta." Antonio said, while smiling.

"Pleasure to meet you." I said, shaking her hand.

I noticed that her hand felt cold and frail. Her hands were smaller than my own. Her eyebrows looked as if they were painted onto her face and her lips only curved slightly as we shook hands, as if she was forcing a smile.

Marcus talked to us for nearly an hour at the hospital. Blanca returned and stared at me intently as Marcus questioned me about my feelings for Antonio. He carried on for so long, that I forgot all about Blanca sitting in the corner, giving me the evil eye.

Antonio noticed that I was uncomfortable and took Catalina and me back to the house. She went into the kitchen to cook us dinner, while we sat together, talking quietly and sipping wine. By the time the food was ready, I could barely stand up straight.

Antonio laughed as he guided me to the dining room, where we quickly ate our food.

When we were finished he walked me up to my room, holding my hand lightly as we walked. We stood outside my door.

"So I know this is a little rushed, but are you willing to be my wife?" Antonio asked. I nodded. He grinned and played with my hand. I wrapped my arms around his neck and smiled up at him.

"You are my angel." I said to him. "I don't know what I'd do without you." Antonio blushed and leaned forward, kissing my lips lightly.

He moved back, studying the expression on my face and then he began to kiss me overpoweringly as he lifted my legs around his waist, leaning me against the hallway wall before carrying me into the bedroom and quietly shutting the door behind him. He forcefully ripped open my blouse, buttons dropping to the floor as he did, while holding my buttocks against him with the other. I tightened my legs around him, as he began putting my breasts in his mouth one at a time, sucking them just hard enough so I felt it and I leaned back, moaning intensely in pleasure.

I could feel his manhood growing, as I clung to him, pushing my buttocks against his waist and leaning back in ecstasy. He lay me down on the bed, kissing me passionately as he removed his shirt. I opened one eye to see sweat glistening from his deeply tanned body. He came at me harder, kissing my breasts again and then moving down to my belly button. I sighed in anticipation, as he lifted my dress slightly with his teeth, leaving my panties exposed in front of his face. I put my hand down to stop him. Antonio laughed and shook his head, his curls beginning to drip with sweat.

He grabbed my hand in his and put it to my chest to keep me from stopping him. He then licked the area around my belly button, going down further and further, as he pulled my panties to the side with his free hand. I leaned my head back.

"Antonio," I whispered, but didn't try to stop him.

This was it. I was in love with him and was ready for him to be my first. I felt my insides going crazy as he stuck out his tongue deep inside of me, moving it around and tasting every inch of me. My body clung to him as he lifted my leg to get in further, causing my body to shudder. I lost control and grabbed a pillow, putting it over my face, so that no one would hear my moans of delight.

He grabbed my butt, pulling it closer to his face and continued to lick my insides quickly, flicking his tongue in and out. I felt myself get hotter and wetter until my head flipped back and I felt a burst of warmth from within. He smiled, getting on top of me, without removing his pants. He kissed me passionately as he rubbed his body against me. I could feel his manhood harden and became uncomfortable as it pressed against me. I wanted him to put it inside of me. I was ready, but instead he slowed down, putting my breast in his mouth and sucking it a few times before kissing me and continuing to play with my bare nipples.

"How bad do you want me Lily?" Antonio asked.

"So bad." I whispered in response, licking my lips and clinging to his strong body as he began to rub himself against me again.

His manhood felt huge against my inner thighs, even while safely in his pants. I didn't dare reach down to touch it, out of fear that I would change my mind about making love to him. He continued to stimulate my body for what felt like hours, suddenly stopping to check his phone. He sighed when he noticed a missed call.

"This is just a taste of what I have to give you the day you become my wife." He said.

I said nothing but gave him a disappointed gaze as he stood up and left the room, leaving me alone to try to comprehend what he had just happened. I was woozy from the wine and fell asleep quickly after he left, dreaming about what could have happened if he had only gone further.

The next day, Antonio acted as if nothing had happened.

We drove with Miguel to pick Elena up at the hospital and all of our discussions were focused on the new baby.

Chapter Ten

The following week, Antonio's uncle came over to invite us to join him and Roberta for dinner at their house. As much as I liked being around Elena and the new baby, I was anxious to get away from Antonio's mother who had also been staying in her house for the past two days. She made it her mission to be around whenever Antonio and I were together, interrupting us when we talked or budging in when he came to sit down next to me.

We quickly said our goodbyes to Elena before happily jumping into Antonio's car, following Marcus home.

We drove for an hour while talking and laughing until we pulled up to a huge Italian villa with the same black cast iron gates surrounding it that Elena had at her home. It was interesting for me to see such lavish homes in Colombia, because the area that my father was from was very poor. I knew that we were not as poor as certain areas of Colombia, such as parts of Tumaco, but in comparison with Antonio and his family, we were definitely poor. I looked back nervously as we drove and saw a navy blue sedan following us and told Antonio. He looked in the side mirror and smiled.

"Oh, that's just Darien and Max." He said. "They're a couple of Uncle Marcus's bodyguards."

When we arrived at Marcus's house, the table was already set with plates of hot food on it. Roberta sat quietly at one end of the table, while Marcus sat directly across from her. Although Marcus spoke English fluently Roberta spoke only a little English. She smiled warmly every so often at me and I did the same. Antonio and his uncle carried out a conversation in Spanish, of which I didn't catch one single word.

"When are you two planning to get married?" Marcus suddenly asked Antonio.

I was slightly taken aback, though Antonio responded quickly and told Marcus and Roberta that we would be married in three months. He looked at me for approval and though I froze for a minute, I nodded my approval and Marcus and Antonio went back to their conversation.

I found myself pushing my rice around and pretending to try and understand what it was that they were talking about. I didn't know why, but suddenly I wasn't happy that Antonio wanted to get married. I thought about how little I had to offer him and felt financially insufficient for him. I also didn't want my father to walk me down the aisle.

"In this short time that I have known you, I can't imagine living one more day without you." Antonio turned to me and said.

I was in shock and could feel my face glow with happiness as he smiled at me.

"I hope that you don't let my family overwhelm you." He said, noticing my anxiety. "From this day forward we are one."

Marcus handed him a box and Antonio pulled out a huge diamond engagement ring. I put my hand to my mouth, in shock. Antonio's smile grew. He slipped it on my finger and I nodded at him, wrapping my arms around his neck and hugging him as soon as it was on. I couldn't believe that he had gotten me a ring. He kissed me on my cheek and told me that he loved me.

Roberta put her hand on her chest in awe. Marcus went to her side and held her close. I looked over at them. Marcus clapped his hands and his butler came with a bottle of champagne and we all had toast after toast. Antonio even drank a little too much but insisted that we needed to leave and that he felt fine. Roberta had the butler bring out coffee and Antonio drank it down in one huge gulp, cringing as he loosened his collar and glanced over at me.

"I live on the side of a mountain." Marcus said. "I'm not going to have you drive off a cliff."

"I'll be fine, Tio." Antonio said again, but Marcus took the keys away from him and Antonio glanced over at me appearing as if he suddenly liked the idea.

Marcus insisted that Antonio leave his car, then motioned for his driver take us back to Elena's.

We walked out to the limousine and no sooner were we seated in the back than Antonio was all over me, kissing me passionately as the driver tried to ignore us.

I felt uncomfortable with the driver watching us kiss, but Antonio acted as though he wasn't there. I could feel his warm hand on my leg working its way up and I pushed him back for a moment. He moved his hand, but began kissing me again harder, this time wrapping his hand around my neck and pulling me toward him until I was the one leaning over him.

Antonio grabbed my leg, trying to move it around him. My tight skirt wasn't cooperating and he quickly became frustrated, lifting it and pulling me to a seated position on top of him, exposing my panties to the driver. Antonio pulled me toward him and cupped each of my buttocks as he kissed me. Once again, I found myself full of desire for him as I lost myself in his kiss.

The driver didn't seem to know whether to stop the car or not as we pulled into Elena's drive way.

Antonio didn't let me go for a minute after we got to the house, continuing to kiss me until we saw his mom and dad leaving in their car.

Antonio quickly thanked the driver, holding my hand and leading me inside the dark house. I leaned against him as we walked, my body turned to him, because I wasn't familiar with Elena's house in the dark. He scooped me up in his strong arms and carried me up the stairs to my room, careful as he took each footstep so that he would not wake anyone up. He set me down in the room, closing the door behind him.

He took a deep breath and staggered a bit as he walked toward me. We began to kiss passionately as we stood in the center of the room. The room began spinning and I clung to him tightly as he grabbed each of my buttocks in his hand, lifting me up and pressing me against the wall while he leaned against me, moving his body up and down against me. I grasped his back tightly, scared that I would fall as we kissed. I was woozy, but felt movement from underneath and realized that he was fondling my panties with his hand. I moaned and suddenly became wet. I put my hand down to try and move his hand away and when I did, he just pressed against them harder. I clung to him as I enjoyed the feeling but tried to stop him again when I felt him sticking one of his fingers inside of me. My eyes got big as I clung to him, not sure of how to react to what I was feeling. Suddenly I didn't want him to stop and he took me to the bed, laying me on the bed and putting his finger to his lips to tell me to be quiet.

I shook my head again as I looked up at him, my head against a soft pillow, but this only made him laugh as he climbed on top of me, kissing me forcefully and sticking his finger inside of me again. He moved it around, playing with the entirety of my insides, watching my body as my breasts raised and lowered with his touch. I looked up at him as I did, feeling embarrassed and hot at the same time. I couldn't control my body and what he was making it do, but I was dizzy from the champagne and wanted him to go further as he watched my facial expressions change.

Finally he stopped and lay down beside me. I rested my head on his chest and clung to his body, neither of us saying a word. He put his arm around me, stroking my shoulder, as if deep in thought.

Antonio smiled and looked into my eyes, telling me that he was Marcus's favorite nephew. Antonio told me that Marcus had bought him his first car, a Chevy Corvette. Antonio was only fourteen years old at the time and Antonio's mother flipped out when she found out about the car. She had yelled at Marcus saying that Antonio couldn't drive it and that this would be way too much money to spend on a present for her son.

Antonio Salvador told him to go ahead and drive the car. Elena was only ten and wanted to come along for the ride so Antonio took her around the town and ended up crashing into a fruit stand. Luckily he hadn't injured anyone in the small village. The car had a few dents when they drove it back, but Marcus just laughed it off. So did Antonio's father. But, Antonio's mother had taken Elena into the house and wouldn't talk to anyone or allow Elena to talk to anyone for a week.

He continued telling me stories about his childhood while I lay in his arms. Antonio's cell phone rang and Antonio stood up to answer it. He walked to the bathroom as he spoke quickly in Spanish.

When he returned he had a huge smile on his face, and he said that Marcus and Roberta decided that they would build us a house as our engagement present. I was in shock.

"Wow," was all that I could say. "That's great."

Antonio didn't seem too surprised. I was feeling a little bubbly and went over to him and kissed him on his neck softly. Immediately he pulled away and opened his mouth to say something, but before he could I kissed him and instead of pulling away he kissed me back only harder and more forcefully than he had before. My skin tingled. Within seconds his hand was pressed against my thighs, slowly inching its way up until it reached the center of my panties. He stroked his hand back and forth and I could feel myself get wet again and let out a moan in pleasure. This seemed to snap Antonio out of it and he shook his head.

"No more liquor for you," he said and backed away.

I felt embarrassed and straightened my skirt out. He lifted my chin in his hand.

"Three months, Lily. I want to do this right." He said as he kissed me lightly on the lips. He stepped out of the room, shutting the door behind him. I threw myself onto the bed angrily and within seconds, completely blacked out.

Chapter Eleven

The next morning both Elena and Antonio's mother were in my room standing over me. I opened one eye and closed it quickly. Blanca glared at me. Her nostrils flared as I slowly opened both eyes. Her short hair was dyed reddish brown, and at the moment it made her look devilish from the glare as the sunlight shined upon it.

"Come on, get ready." Elena said. "You and my Mother are going shopping after lunch."

Antonio's mother shot me a disgruntled look and they both left the room.

I really didn't want to wake up. I had a slight headache and my stomach felt bubbly. I slowly moved to my side to check the time. It was already eleven o'clock in the morning. I pulled myself from the bed and took a quick shower. I put a pair of tight blue jeans on and a fitted white tee-shirt. I pulled the top half of my hair up in a ponytail smiling down at my ring as I did. I felt as if I was living in a dream.

When I went downstairs, Antonio's immediate family was sitting down in the living room drinking coffee and deep in a conversation. I stood at the doorway trying to make out what they were talking about and blushed as soon as they noticed that I entered the room. Antonio walked across the room to greet me, putting his arm around me after giving me a quick peck on the lips.

"Ya, cálmate todos." Antonio said loudly. "We'll finish this discussion later."

He irritably kissed the side of my head, leaving me with the impression that they were talking about me. Blanca looked as though she was about to shriek, but no one paid any attention to her and instead stood up and went to the dining room. Antonio shot me a look with raised eyebrows and kissed my cheek again, this time he pulled me close and laughed.

"Everyone's in a bad mood today." Antonio said quietly to me. "How do you feel?"

"I slept well." I smiled naughtily at him. He laughed loudly, which made me laugh. Everyone turned to look at us.

"See Lily, this is just what I need." He said. "Someone who makes me laugh." He took my hand and kissed it, as he glanced around the room. No sooner did he look up then his mother erupted in madness.

"Tú no sabes lo que estás haciendo!" Blanca exclaimed from across the table. "You cannot marry this girl."

Blanca looked beside herself as she glanced to the others for support. When no one came to her side, her eyes lit with furry, determined to bring everyone else's moods down with her.

"You know her father is trash." She said through her teeth. "I thought that I taught you better."

Elena glanced across the table at me with apologetic eyes. I looked down at the table cloth. Antonio put his hand on his head, showing that he was extremely angry, grabbing his hair and pulling it as though he was trying to hold himself back.

"¿Cómo te atreves a insultar a ella!" He shouted across the table at her. Antonio Salvador glanced over at his wife angrily and gave her a hand signal to tell her to stop. Catalina quickly put food in front of me and touched my shoulder, as if to say remain calm.

I took a bite of a sandwich made from plantains and chewed it very slowly looking down at my fork as Catalina served everyone else their plates. Antonio sat beside me fuming, looking as if he was ready to explode. I knew that there was only a matter of time before either of them would go at it again. Elena sat at the head of the table, giving Blanca an expression that told me that she was upset, but not surprised with her.

A few heads turned my way as I let out a sigh inadvertently. I tried my best to make it seem like it was an accident, but I noticed that Antonio gritted his teeth as he stared at his mother, waiting for her to say something else. There was absolute quiet throughout the room.

If this wasn't the quiet before the storm, I don't know what was. I could almost feel the thinness in the air. Suddenly Blanca exploded in Spanish. She spoke very quickly and in a low angry tone, standing up as she spoke. Antonio stood up and yelled at her in Spanish, apparently getting his point across as she pressed her lips together furiously.

Antonio Salvador stood up, holding the back of his hand to Antonio's chest and Antonio sat back down irritably. Blanca sat in her seat with tears in her eyes. Again, there was complete silence.

I tried to catch Antonio's eye so that I could smile at him, but he would not take his eyes off his mother.

"I think it's a good idea." Elena said slowly, but loud enough that everyone heard her.

"It's a little quick, but sometimes it's better to get married quickly, before either person changes their mind." Elena finished off.

Miguel shot her a deadly expression and she quickly began to eat her lunch. I knew that Elena had told Miguel several times that if they had the chance to do everything over again, she would have run away. His love for her was more of a brotherly love, she had told me. As I glanced across the table at the two of them, I wondered if they had ever been as happy as Antonio and I were.

I watched Roberta, who nodded at Marcus as he ate his food. He looked like he was eating his food as fast as he could to avoid getting into the conversation. He grimaced as she said something to Blanca in Spanish. Miguel immediately shot something back, as if he was guarding Blanca and then the entire table went at it again. I looked back and forth at them as they took turns speaking. It was as if I were watching a ping pong match.

"This is ridiculous." Marcus finally said. "We'll pay for everything. Carajo, he's my godson. End of story. Can we eat?"

Blanca stared at him with a dismayed expression. Antonio Salvador threw his hand down on the table, avoiding his wife's gaze.

"No." Antonio's Salvador said. "We will pay for the wedding! You're doing enough already." He stood up and paced the room. "It's only right." Antonio Salvador continued. "It's my son. Al diablo con lo que mi esposa dice."

Blanca pressed her lips together and then exploded again in Spanish. This time she directed her anger at her husband. She huffed as she crossed her arms against her chest glaring sullenly across the table at us.

Antonio ate a bite of his sandwich and then threw it on his plate, standing up. "Cállate ya!" Antonio said, wiping his face before leaning across the table as he spoke. "Everything's always about money with you. I'll pay for the wedding. It's not like I don't have money."

He sat down. A fierce look appeared on his face, as he pushed his plate away. "I cannot stand this arguing, Ma." He said. "I did not come home to argue!" He paused, finally looking over at me as I forced a smile. "I love Lily and she loves me and that's all that matters right now."

Blanca sighed. At first she did not look up at him, but then she slowly raised her head and glanced from him to me, making it obvious that she was waiting for me to respond. I nodded at her.

"It's true Mrs. Valencia." I said, looking her directly in the eye as I spoke. "I'm in love with your son."

She looked down momentarily, but I wasn't ready to give her the satisfaction of getting away from guilt that easily.

"From the moment I met him, I knew that I could never be without him. I didn't know who he was, but even if I had known, I don't think that it would have made a difference."

Antonio took my hand in his and stroked it. I was shaking. I had never spoken out of turn to an adult and I was not used to speaking to so many people at one time about my feelings. I felt that I needed to let her know how I felt about her son. Nobody said anything for a while. There was a quiet clang of glasses being set down on the table as everyone took a sip of their drinks. Catalina quickly gathered the plates and passed out seconds to those that nodded. Miguel and Antonio Salvador were the only ones who asked for more food. Everyone else seemed to wonder if the fight was over as they sat quietly in their chairs.

"Ella es solo una chica." Blanca said slowly through her teeth. "She doesn't know what she wants."

"Ya!" Antonio shot at her. "Leave it alone."

I glanced over at him as he glared at her. I began to gather all of the courage that I had inside of me, to speak once again.

"Mrs. Valencia," I said. "You know, I don't really know anything about the whole wedding thing. Would there be a possibility that you could plan our wedding for us?"

Everyone glanced over at me with wide eyes, including Blanca. This was exactly what I had been shooting for. I could feel the triumph ring throughout my body. Antonio nearly choked on what he was chewing and when he was done coughing, everyone's attention turned back to Blanca.

"You're in Colombia now Lily-Anne." She said coldly, purposely pronouncing my name wrong. "You are supposed to say Señora and Señor, not Mr. and Mrs."

She let out a forced laugh. She turned to Miguel for approval.

"My son wants to marry some girl that doesn't know how to speak properly in English or Spanish." She said under her breath, loud enough for all of us to hear .

107

I felt burned and immediately regretted trying to befriend her at all as I looked away from Miguel's gaze. I eyed her as I sipped on a glass of water. Antonio and his father both glared at her with unforgiving eyes. Elena cleared her throat. Blanca rearranged herself in the chair.

"You trust my decisions then?" Blanca blurted out against her will, surprising everyone as she spoke.

"Yes." I responded coldly. "I give you my permission to plan everything."

I sighed, as I slouched down in my chair. Antonio put his hand reassuringly on my thigh. I glanced at him and smiled.

"I really don't care if there are ten people there, or a hundred people there." I said, pressing my lips together. "Of course I want everything to be appropriate and since I don't have an idea of what an appropriate wedding is, you can handle all the arrangements."

Blanca sat thoughtfully in her chair for a moment. The table was quiet as everyone waited for her response. I tried to show that I didn't care what her response was, by taking another bite of my sandwich, not looking at her as I did. I looked up after swallowing my food and noticed that a smile was slowly appearing on her face.

"Well three months is a short time to plan a wedding." Blanca said, shooting Antonio a concerned expression. "However, I will accept your challenge."

A genuine smile appeared on Antonio's face as he glanced from me to his father.

"My wife does like to plan parties." Antonio Salvador said standing up to walk behind his wife and rested his hands on her shoulders.

"This is the best news I've heard all day." Antonio Salvador said. "I'm happy for my family and all of my future family members."

"A toast." Marcus said, standing up.

"You and your toasts." Antonio replied, laughing. "We're going to turn Lily into an alcoholic."

Everyone at the table laughed and Antonio rubbed my leg under the table. I tried not to look surprised as his hand went higher and higher up my leg. Just as I got goosebumps, he stopped. All the tension seemed to leave the table immediately. Everyone laughed and joked with one another. I felt relieved. I had just been accepted into a new family.

After lunch was over, Antonio Salvador stood up and motioned to the other men to wrap it up. I glanced out to the backyard and saw three men being shown to the patio tables by Catalina. Antonio stood up and said goodbye to me, bending over to kiss me on the cheek. He took out a bill from his wallet and slipped it into my side pocket.

"In case you see anything that you like." He said. I nodded, but didn't look at what he had slipped in.

"I love you." He said, lifting my hand and holding it for a minute before pulling away.

"I love you too." I responded softly. Elena quickly grabbed my hand and pulled me to the front door.

"I decided to come with you." She said happily.

"Are you sure?" I asked. I knew that this was the first time that she would be leaving the house after she had the baby. She already had a new nanny and the nanny spent most of her time with the baby, but if Elena could really come with us, I would feel much better, I thought.

We walked to her limo and got in. Blanca was already inside waiting impatiently. The driver began to drive as soon as Elena shut the door.

"It took you girls long enough." Blanca said snidely. Her tone quickly changed.

"I love to shop." Blanca exclaimed with a huge accent. "This is going to be difficult. We have a lot of ground to cover today." Elena and I shot each other looks.

"Yes, she's always like this." Elena laughed raising her eyebrows, referring to her mother's sudden mood change.

I raised my eyebrows back at her, being careful not to let Blanca see me do it.

Even though I had been good friends with Elena for three years, none of what was happening felt real. Never would I have imagined that I would end up with Elena's brother. I thought back to just three weeks before when I had cursed my life as I walked home from work. Now, I didn't know if I would ever have to work again.

Blanca broke the silence telling us all of the stores that we were going to. She had a check list all prepared and held it up. "Can you believe that I wrote all of this down while you girls were inside?" She asked. "I figured we could begin getting you ready for the wedding and of course, get you some new clothes." She laughed, directing the last statement at Elena.

"Do you like purple or blue better?" Blanca asked me without waiting for an answer. "Silver!" She exclaimed, her face lighting up as she jotted it down.

Blanca had completely changed her attitude toward me in the matter of minutes. It was daunting. She was entirely too energized for me as she rushed us from store to store. I was in shock at first, because I didn't realize that many of the stores we went to even existed in Colombia. I felt that the time I had spent living with my father had caused me to become isolated from the rest of the world. We were in the city that I had never seen. There was a church with a high tower in the middle of the town and young boys walked in groups with skateboards in hand.

Blanca bought both Elena and me a bunch of clothes, even stopping in one shop to get ideas for my wedding dress. While we were there she insisted that I be measured, ordered the invitations for the wedding to be printed that day, and also picked out the style of the dress that the bridesmaids would wear. Although this city was a good distance from where we lived, it seemed like the woman who ran the store knew who Blanca and Elena were. The woman questioned Blanca about me, who told her simply that her son had decided to marry me.

We did so much shopping that my head felt as if it was spinning. When we got to the dress shop to pick up the invitations, they were closed but a man stood outside with a box, waiting for us. The driver got out and took the box and put it in the front of the car with him. Blanca gave her thanks from the window, as we drove off and into the night. I wondered how long the man had stood out there waiting for us, as I gazed up at the dark sky. Elena's cell phone rang and she talked quietly to Miguel, letting him know that we were on our way home.

No sooner did she hang up than Blanca's attitude change again. She sat with her body planted firmly in her seat. She looked like she was attempting to hold herself back from what she was about to ask me. Elena glanced at her nervously as she watched her.

"Are you a virgin?" Blanca blatantly asked. Elena put her hand to her mouth in disbelief as she glanced over at the driver.

"Yes." I said without hesitation, although I was shocked at the question.

"I don't believe you." Blanca replied, pressing her lips together. My mouth dropped open, I was in shock. I had finally begun to think that she liked me, how could her attitude change so quickly?

"Mother, stop it. Antonio already knows that she is a virgin, you know that." Elena said something in Spanish to her. I could tell that it was something about my mother dying before she had the chance to talk to me about sex. The limo seemed silent for a moment while Blanca thought over whatever it was that Elena had said. Blanca shook her head a couple of minutes later, suddenly feeling sorry for me.

"When it's your first time it will be very painful." She explained. "Your body will stretch to make space for his manhood and you will feel your body begin to rip apart. You may even bleed."

I winced, closing my legs tightly and sinking back in my chair. If there was blood involved, it had to be painful, I thought.

"It will be very painful the first time." Blanca said again. "After a time, you will enjoy it."

Blanca sat quietly for a minute. Suddenly Elena's words about my mother had left her thoughts.

"My sister said that there is a rumor going on about you." Blanca said. "You were seen with your father and a pimp in the village. Is this true?"

I stared at her, not knowing how to respond.

"I want to prove to everyone, including my sister, that it is not true." Blanca said.

Elena shook her head and looked out the window.

Blanca took my hands in hers. "You have to do something for me, so Antonio doesn't look like a fool for marrying you." Blanca said, sighing heavily as she let my hands go.

I did not respond. I didn't like the idea, but I didn't want Antonio to look like a fool either. "What do you want me to do?" I asked.

"I'll tell you on your wedding night." Blanca responded.

When we got back to Elena's house, the driver let Elena and me off at the front door. Catalina came out to get the bags, insisting that I not help her. I thanked Blanca for everything and surprisingly, she kissed my cheek.

"Think about what I said." She whispered to me.

I nodded at her and stepped away from the car. Then the driver drove off to take her home.

Catalina told us that Antonio was waiting inside. I hurried in and paused when I saw him. He stood at the end of the entry hall with a troubled expression on his face.

"What's wrong Antonio?" I asked, walking over to him and touching his elbow lightly.

"I've been waiting since six o'clock for you." He replied harshly. "I wanted to take you out to dinner."

"I'm sorry, Antonio." I said. "I wanted to get back here to be with you, too. There was just so much to do. Your mother is going all out with this wedding planning idea."

He remained quiet, so I went on to tell him about the city that we were in and all of the stores that we went to, about the dress, the invitations and how happy his mother seemed to be. He listened to me tell the story with a frustrated expression on his face. Finally he grinned at me.

"Uncle Marcus took me with him to buy the house today!" He exclaimed suddenly. "He's going to have it remodeled. It's not huge, but it's good for now."

"Ooh, let's go see it." I said, pulling him towards toward the door.

"Not today, Lily." He replied. "Not until it is done."

He gave me a kiss on the cheek and walked out the front door.

I was in shock. He hadn't even said goodbye, I thought to myself. I wondered what was wrong with him. I walked over to the window and looked out just in time to see him drive off. I stood at the window, sulking momentarily and then walked over to hold the door open for Catalina as she brought in the last bag.

"What's wrong child?" She asked when she saw my disturbed expression.

"I don't know what just happened." I replied. "I think Antonio is mad at me."

"He's not mad at you." Catalina replied.

She looked around the room before continuing.

"When you are married to one of them," she motioned upstairs with her chin, as if to point out Miguel. "You make your schedule around theirs, not your own."

She smiled back at me as she walked into the kitchen.

Chapter Twelve

For the next two months, I asked Antonio to take me to visit our new home. He denied my requests, saying only that he wanted everything to look perfect before I saw it. I was growing impatient because Antonio was practically avoiding me. I knew that he was adding all of the finishing touches on the house, but with that and his meetings every morning, I hardly ever had the chance to spend time with him. When we spent time around each other, his family was constantly interrupting us and pulling either him or me in different directions for our opinions on plans for the wedding.

While Antonio seemed to be excited about the wedding in front of the family, he didn't say one word about it to me directly. He made an effort to purposely not spend any time alone with me so that we wouldn't tempt ourselves before our wedding. I was growing visibly annoyed with him and I was worried that he saw the change in my attitude. Elena was busy helping her mother plan the wedding and I began to feel like everyone had forgotten about me. I often spent my days reading books, or talking with Catalina in the kitchen.

One afternoon Elena and Blanca informed me that they had been in contact with my father and that Madrigal would be allowed to be one of my bridesmaids. They said that my father also confirmed that he would walk me down the aisle. Although both Elena and Blanca had smiles on their faces when relaying the news to me, I felt my heart drop. I wasn't sure that I ever wanted to see my father again. They asked if there was anyone besides my father and his family that I wanted to invite and I thought of my Aunt Maria. Blanca promised to call her as she rushed Elena upstairs to work on our seating arrangements.

I was excited about my life with Antonio, but I began to wonder if he felt the same way toward me. He appeared to be stressed out over the course of the last two months. Finally, as the house was nearly finished, he started spending more time with me. It happened as quickly as Chicago changes weather. He popped up one morning while I was sleeping, waking me by kissing my neck and after that he was there every day, making me feel loved and wanted once again.

With every day that passed in the month leading up to our wedding, he took me somewhere special and did something nice for me. I told him every day that I could not wait to be his wife as we spent the entire afternoon talking about our lives with one another. He told me that he wanted us to have at least four children. I agreed with him and told him that my dream was to go back to school and he agreed to be supportive of that.

During that month, I became so close to him I felt like he was like my best friend and lover combined. Our souls seemed to have joined as one. I often knew what he was going to say, before he said it and when he kissed me, I felt like I exploded with unbelievable desire for him. He knew the power that he had over me. He played with my emotions in that way, passionately kissing me, squeezing my breasts and touching me between my legs until he felt my panties get hot and wet.

He would stand up and adjust his manhood in front of me, making it obvious to me that he was well endowed. I could feel my insides tighten with desire when he did but, his size made me wonder if I was going to be able to handle him. I respected him for wanting to wait until we got married before having sex. The fact of the matter was that I didn't think that I was ready for him anyhow. I wondered what would happen if he didn't pull away. Would I be strong enough to stop him on my own?

One morning when I opened my eyes he was at my bedside smiling at me as I slept. My eyes fluttered open and I covered my face with my hands.

"My God, Antonio," I said laughing. "How long have you been there?"

"Not long enough," he replied. "Come on, get ready. I have a surprise for you." He left the room as I giggled.

I wondered what the surprise was. I quickly showered, dressed and went downstairs. Antonio came to my side and wrapped his arms around my waist, holding me tightly before pulling a blindfold from his pocket. I gasped as I wondered what he had planned for us.

"No peeking," he said as he blindfolded me.

"Where are we going?"

He did not respond. I could imagine him smiling as he led me out to his car. We drove for about ten minutes in complete silence. He didn't even turn the radio on as we drove, but I don't think either of us noticed the silence. He was excited about my reaction as he drove and I sat quietly in anticipation.

He finally stopped the car and lifted my blindfold.

When I opened my eyes, I saw a large house with a black wrought iron fence around it. If I looked to either side I saw nothing but forest. Behind us, there was a long driveway that stretched downhill to a road that led to the town square. I could see some of the vendors clearly watching us in the distance. I climbed out of the car and stood on the cement driveway, turning around and realizing that the house overlooked a church. It appeared far away as the house was situated on the side of a mountain.

"This is ours." Antonio said, a smile appearing on his face.

"No way," I replied in shock.

Three men stood at the gate. Each of them had guns strapped to their side. For some reason the sight of them bothered me. Every one of Antonio's relatives needed guards for their house. I didn't think anything of it until now, but our guards in particular alarmed me. Two were dressed the same, wearing uniforms and hats, while the other was dressed in plain clothes. The plainclothes officer was big, at least 270 pounds and well over six feet tall. All of the men wore dark glasses and earpieces.

"Gilbert!" Antonio called out to the big man. "Let me introduce you to my future wife."

Gilbert walked over to where I stood. His size definitely intimidated me as I looked up at him. I stepped back as he came toward me, not because I was afraid, but just so I could see him better as he stood before me.

"Pleasure to meet you." Gilbert said. He shook my hand firmly, a gentle smile appearing on his face.

"Gilbert is my new body guard." Antonio said.

My eyebrows rose as he spoke. Gilbert and my eyes met momentarily, before I refocused on Antonio.

"Antonio, what do you need a bodyguard for?" I asked.

"For protection." Antonio replied firmly, putting his arm around me as he spoke.

I suddenly began to feel nervous. What had I gotten myself into? I was sure that Antonio noticed the worried look on my face, but apparently, my worry wasn't a concern for him at this point in our relationship. Antonio smiled and exchanged glances with Gilbert.

"Don't worry." Antonio said. "It's a job."

Antonio looked at me closely and his face softened slightly. "We all have to do something." He turned and motioned for me to follow him to the garage as he began to walk toward it.

I reluctantly followed, looking back at his car and wondering what was to become of my life. I knew there were several important questions that I'd never taken the time to get specific answers for. One of those important questions being, what he did for a living.

All of my worry was taken away as I walked into the garage and felt overcome by excitement. "Wow! We could fit four cars in here!" I exclaimed.

Antonio smiled with relief as I quickly forgot about his bodyguard.

"Yes and one of them will be yours as soon as you learn how to drive." Antonio replied. "When you do learn, you are not to leave without me."

Antonio looked at me and smiled mischievously.

"Understand?" Antonio asked.

I glanced up at him, not knowing how to take his comment. I nodded worriedly at him. His face immediately filled with warmth as he sensed my fear.

"I can't have anything happen to my princess." He said.

I laughed lightly, still feeling some nervousness.

He picked me up in his arms and carried me inside of the adjoining door to the house. I forced a smile as I looked into his eyes and then kissed him as we entered the kitchen. He set me down on my feet on a black and white tiled floor, where two older ladies in uniforms stood. Gilbert walked slowly to the side of the room, as if attempting to be out of sight.

"This is Melissa, the Maid and Rosa, the Cook." Antonio said, nodding at the two women.

They nodded and smiled at me. Something told me that their smiles were not genuine, but I nodded back at them as they stood before me. A man cleared his throat and we turned to see an older man standing in the doorway. He was thin and darker than the two women, but their faces shared the same features.

"This is Charles." Antonio said. "He is Melissa and Rosa's brother and has worked for my family all of my life. He will be your driver whenever I'm not around."

Charles stepped forward and we shook hands. I felt uncomfortable as I stood before the three. I felt as if all three were sizing me up. I stood next to Antonio, relieved when he finally led me on to the next room and nodded back at them as we left.

Antonio kissed me on the cheek as we walked through the house. I clung to his arm as he discussed changes that he'd made to each room. Antonio explained that Charles had a room in the house with us. He was divorced and his children lived in Venezuela. Melissa and Rosa lived a few miles down the road and had their own families. Melissa had three young children. Charles's room was on the first floor, near the kitchen. Antonio explained that upstairs there were four guest bedrooms and our master bedroom. Each bedroom had a bathroom of its own and Antonio said the house was just something for now and that he wanted something bigger in the future.

The house was elegantly decorated. We stood in the foyer of the house looking back at the living room, which boasted a fireplace with a handcrafted mantel. The staircase leading to our room was beautiful. It wound up in a spiral straight to a loft lookout.

"I love the stairway!" I exclaimed.

Antonio nodded in agreement and followed me as I made my way up the stairs.

"There is a second stairway in the back hallway that you can use, if you want to go down to the kitchen." He explained. "This one is more for show."

As I walked up the stairs, he gave my butt a squeeze while Gilbert and Charles watched and laughed lightly. I jumped and turned to look at him.

"I just couldn't help myself." He said smiling back at the other men.

I smiled at him, shaking my finger and feeling a little embarrassed.

We continued up the stairs and he stepped out in front of me, leading me straight to our bedroom. We had a great view of the entire village from our bedroom. The room had a balcony that extended in a semi-circle over the front yard and had space for chairs and a table. He led me over to it and I stepped out to check out the view. It overlooked the town square and I felt happy to be able to stand and watch people in the far distance, shopping below us. He smiled, stepping out with me and wrapping his hands around my waist. We stood there for a few moments, before stepping back inside of our room.

Our room was very plain. Antonio had decorated the room entirely in white. There were no pictures on the wall and it appeared that the sole purpose of this room would be to sleep in. I was sure that once we'd taken more pictures, he'd allow me to put some up along the bare walls.

"My version of innocence." Antonio said as I looked around in awe.

I put my hand down on the bed and was surprised by its softness. I quickly climbed onto it, laying back and allowing my body to sink into it. I closed my eyes as he lay down beside me and began stroking my hair. We both drifted off into a short nap awaken by the sound of his cell phone ringing.

"Oh crap!" He said, looking at the phone and then jumping up, running over to the balcony and looking over the side.

"I'm up here," he said loudly, while waving.

He came back into the room and lifted my hand.

"I have to go to a meeting." He said. "I'm sorry, I completely forgot."

"Can I come?" I asked.

"No, are you crazy," he asked. "I can't have my woman there."

I gave him a sulky look and followed him downstairs, where he found Charles and asked him to take me back to Elena's house. I watched as he got back into his own car with Gilbert and sped away.

I climbed into the car with Charles, trying not to let my sadness show as I did.

"You know it kills him, every time he has to leave you." Charles said to me from the front seat. "He thinks something is going to happen and you won't be there when he gets back."

"That's silly." I replied.

"Don't say that it's silly." Charles replied. "There are a lot of bad people in this world."

We sat in silence for a few moments as Charles drove.

"My first wife and children were killed years ago, by a group of men that came into our home when I wasn't home." Charles said, glancing back at me to shoot me a convincing expression.

I thought about what he said and how to react. I sat silently as we drove. At the time I wasn't sure that I believed him, but Antonio became more protective of me over the next month. He didn't want me to leave Elena's house unless it was completely necessary and when I did mention that I wanted to leave, as far as he was concerned, it was not necessary. I felt comfortable at her house because as our wedding approached there were so many people around to keep my mind busy.

Everyone else was doing the work of planning for our wedding, allowing Antonio and I time to enjoy each other whenever we had the chance to. Antonio took me out to the backyard everyday just to get away from the madness inside. Blanca was going absolutely nuts. She was yelling at everyone that came within two feet of her. She made Elena cry on several occasions. Blanca wanted everything to be perfect and no one was doing their part as far as she was concerned. She insisted that everyone around her get their act together.

Blanca had decided the wedding would be a major event, the reception was to be held across town and I knew nothing of what was planned for it. Blanca designated herself a room in Elena's house that was off limits to everyone, including Elena. Blanca locked herself in the room for hours, making phone calls to different people. She always came out muttering about only having three months to plan a wedding.

Finally with just two days before our wedding, all of the women in my wedding party were going to meet and try on their dresses. I was anxious and uneasy at the same time. I felt like the world was spinning faster and faster around me. Blanca insisted that Antonio and I weren't to spend any more time together after we left. Antonio agreed and gave me a cell phone to keep so that he could call me instead.

Having a cell phone was new to me, but it allowed me to be closer to him. The problem was that he began to call every fifteen minutes which began to make me feel anxiety build up, though I didn't dare tell him that. I sat, talking to him, telling him what everyone was doing and he questioned me about what I told him. Soon I began to feel frustrated. I couldn't understand what was making him be like this. I told myself that it was everyone else that was getting to me.

I sat next to Blanca watching as Roberta, Elena and a couple of Elena's cousins ran into fitting rooms, trying on their dresses and coming out for Blanca's approval. Blanca finally decided that the ladies looked decent and told me that it was my turn to try my dress on. Antonio called me for the fifth time right at that minute and Blanca grabbed the phone from my ear. She screamed something in Spanish at him and slammed the phone shut. She wiped sweat from her forehead and turned the phone over, removing the battery and throwing it into her purse. She pulled out a mirror and studied her eyes.

"I think I am getting wrinkles," she said.

I let out a small laugh and stood up. It was my turn. I was nervous because I had not seen my dress. All of the women gathered around me as the clerk brought out the dress and dressed me. They all stepped forward, pulling zippers and strings and hooks, until the clerk brought over a full length mirror.

I stood in front of the mirror admiring myself. The dress was beautiful. It had white pearls with embroidered designs all over. I stood there, starting at myself in awe, running my hands down the silky sides of it. I could hear the women in the background commenting on how beautiful and elegant the dress was. Blanca nodded happily as Elena's phone rang.

"Antonio." Elena said to her mother and rolled her eyes.

She answered the phone and began to hand it to me and when Blanca grabbed the phone and scolded Antonio in Spanish. He must have said something back, because Blanca was furious.

"You call her back tomorrow!" She said loudly into the phone. "No you can't see her. No don't you dare come over. I swear if you come over I am canceling the wedding." She finally hung up on him, shaking her head. "Unbelievable," she muttered.

Antonio did not call back again that night and my tension rose. I took off the dress with the other women's help, anticipating the moment I would be able to put it on again. We all got back into the car and went back to Elena's house for dinner.

The drive home consisted of everyone gushing about the dresses and how beautiful they were. Blanca seemed pleased and sat tall in her seat, beaming with pride. She had lost at least twenty pounds during the planning of Antonio and my wedding and was joking about how she was ready to plan another one. As I watched her, I began to wonder if she was sincere in wishing us happiness. I tried to remember that she had done so much for us in the planning of the wedding. I felt as though something inside of me was telling me that I couldn't trust her.

I felt incredibly nervous about becoming Antonio's wife the day after tomorrow. I wished that I would be able to see him that night. I knew that he would be able to calm me down. Although I wasn't the one planning the wedding, I was positive that something was going to go wrong.

Finally we arrived at Elena's house and everyone piled out of the car, walking toward the house and smiling at me suspiciously. Catalina was already at the door and also had a suspicious expression as she ushered us in. I began to wonder what was going on. No sooner did I step foot into the entry hall then about fifty women holding champagne appeared in the foyer.

"Surprise." Everyone screamed.

I looked around at faces that I did not know and obscene decorations everywhere.

"Oh my Goodness." I said under my breath. "What if the kids see this?"

"They are at Uncle Javier's house today." Elena answered quickly as she pulled me to the middle of the crowd.

"We couldn't let you get married without a bachelorette party." She shouted as everyone cheered.

Is this what Antonio was so nervous about, I wondered. Blanca blushed and went over to talk with her sister, Juana, and her niece, Yasmin. Elena handed me a drink with an obscene straw to celebrate the occasion and then pulled me around the room to introduce me to everyone. Most of the women were Elena's extended family. There were so quite a few aunts and cousins as well as two of Elena's old friends from school. Neither of them was married, though both were very pretty. Her friends crowned me with a tiara with condoms glued to a veil coming out of the back.

125

Liliana

I blushed heavily as Catalina's three daughters came out to help her serve everyone. I felt uncomfortable at the party and even weirder to see that all the food was themed for the party. There were different kinds of sausages and sculpted cheese being served for appetizers, and my cake was in the shape of a man with a penis extending from the top of it!

Elena had me sit in a throne in the front of the room and soon I felt overwhelmed because everyone kept bringing me shot glasses, insisting that I drink with them. I laughed at the games Elena had the women play and the room began to spin.

I did not even notice that a police officer had entered the room as the lights went out and disco lights and a flashing white light replaced them. The police officer pulled me to my feet and led me as I staggered to the middle of the room where he told me to hold on to his shirt and when I did he moved back so fast that his clothes came off in my hand. I blushed and frantically looked for a corner to hide in. Elena, Yasmin, and Elena's friends cheered me on, as the policeman, now dressed only in Speedos, was dancing all around me and over me. He put whipped cream on his chest and suggested that I lick it off. I shook my head and a few people groaned and tried to coax me into doing it.

He smiled and danced a little more for me and then sat me in my throne of humiliation as he danced in front of me for the next five minutes. The policeman did splits and all kinds of seductive moves around me and on my chair. He told me to spank his butt if I wanted him to leave me alone and I did hesitantly, bringing on plenty of cheers. He began to pull the other women to the center of the room and danced with them one by one as the rest of us watched in shock at some of the things that they were doing. I glanced over at Blanca and her sister who were surprisingly laughing and encouraging the other women to go out and dance with him. Roberta even danced with him for a while.

When the party was over, Catalina's daughters stayed to clean up, and Elena came up to my room with me.

We lay on my bed and talked about the party, until we fell asleep, at four o'clock in the morning. I felt Elena try to wake me up for breakfast, but I fell back to sleep and slept most of the day.

When I finally woke up and came downstairs, Elena and Blanca were sitting down to lunch with the baby. I wiped the sleep from my eyes as I entered the room and smiled nervously, trying to remember what had happened the night before. Elena smiled.

Blanca turned to me immediately as I sat down. "Your cell phone has been ringing all morning." She said to me angrily. "I told Antonio to calm down, but the man is going crazy. He says he is coming over after their meeting. I cannot stop him, you have to call him and talk some sense into him."

"But, I want to see him too." I whined. I felt like I was going crazy without him.

Blanca shook her head at Elena. "It is bad luck, I am telling you." Blanca said.

Blanca stood up and walked over to my side.

"You call him and tell him not to come." She ordered.

"Fine, I'll call him." I said obediently, as I tried to remain calm.

Blanca smiled and handed me the phone.

No sooner did she hand me the phone than Antonio came bursting through the front door, followed by Miguel and his father. Blanca stood up and tried to keep Antonio from entering the room, but it was too late, because I found myself running to him and into his arms as he pushed her away. Antonio Salvador smiled and held his arms out as if to say he had nothing to do with it. Blanca tried to pull us apart but Antonio wouldn't let her. Elena burst out laughing and Miguel came to pick up Miguel Jr. and play with him.

Catalina brought a cart of food from the kitchen and everyone sat down to eat.

Antonio held my hand tightly in his, not letting go even to eat. He struggled to use his left hand and had some near misses. Blanca sat scolding everyone in Spanish. She even grumbled at Catalina, insisting that she, too, was in on everything.

When everyone was done eating, Antonio yelled at his sister for giving me the bachelorette party. He was furious that she had a stripper there and Miguel glanced over at her, pretending to be surprised.

"The stripper was Mom's idea, okay, Antonio!" Elena said fiercely.

All heads turned to Blanca who blushed and put her hands up, speechless.

Antonio looked like a bomb waiting to explode, he was so mad. His hand gripped mine tightly.

Elena stared across the table at him as she chewed her last bite. "Anyway," Elena said loudly. "It's not like you didn't have strippers at your bachelor party. I heard all about you and the blonde."

Antonio looked like he had just swallowed his tongue and shot Elena an expression that was frightful. I dropped my hand from his grasp, but he immediately reached for it and held it even tighter than before, as I stared at him.

"Nothing happened." He said to me, looking into my eyes.

I nodded and the table remained quiet. He shot Elena a horrible expression and she raised her eyebrows at him, calling for Catalina to clear the plates.

Antonio took me into the other room after lunch. He wanted to leave with me, but Blanca wouldn't allow it. I suddenly felt uncomfortable around him and tried to distance myself from him as we stood alone in Miguel's study.

"Why didn't you tell me about your bachelor party?" I asked.

"Because, I knew that they were planning yours and I thought that I'd ruin the surprise if I told you about mine." He said, trying to kiss me as he followed me around the room.

I moved away from him and stared blankly at the wall.

He put his hand on my chin, turning my face to him. "Lily, I love you and only you." He said convincingly.

Although we stood in Miguel's study with the door open, he began to kiss me forcefully, slamming the door shut.

I heard Blanca begin to scream at the others about being left alone together before the wedding, but everyone tried to calm her down.

Antonio didn't stop kissing me as he pulled me close and didn't let me go, despite me trying to back away from him. I heard Antonio Salvador suggest that they all go outside and finally there was quiet as Antonio kissed me forcefully, lifting me up and then laying me down on the floor.

"What are you doing?" I nervously asked him as I glanced around the room at the windows with the curtains wide open. I was sure that one of the others would walk by at any minute.

Antonio laughed at my nervousness, smiling coyly as he fought with me to remove my panties from under my skirt. He lay down on the side of me, continuing to kiss me forcefully as his hand went from my knee to the inside of my thigh, quickly, despite me trying to push his hand away. He played with me for a while before sticking his finger deep inside of me. I froze against the hard wood floor and moaned as he muffled my moan with a kiss. As I got wetter, he tried to stick two fingers in and I winced and put my hand to his chest and pushed him away. He quickly stood up and walked across the room.

"Just checking." He said and walked out of the room, leaving me and my panties sprawled out on the floor in shock as I scrambled to get them on quickly.

Liliana

I heard Antonio go outside and begin to yell at his mother about what he would have done if anything would have happened. I was embarrassed and angry. I ran up to my room as everyone came inside, and I locked myself in.

Antonio came to the door but I wouldn't answer him as he knocked. I lay with my face buried in a pillow while tears fell from the corners of my eyes. Two minutes later, he opened the locked door and quietly came inside. He came to my side and tried to make me laugh.

"The wedding is off." I said to him, through tears of rage. "How dare you embarrass me like that?"

"Sweetheart, your innocence is very important to me." He said as he rubbed my back. "It's one of the reasons I'm marrying you."

I lay still without answering him as he began to massage my entire body.

"You're different than the rest of the women here." He explained. "Some of these women have been with who knows how many men. Don't you understand?"

I didn't look at him. I just lay in the bed staring at the wall, as he continued to caress my body. It felt good, but I wasn't giving in. He lay down in the bed with me, trying hard to get me to look at him, but I wouldn't. I was so mad that I didn't even notice that his mother standing at the bedside as he tried to console me. He kissed my cheek over and over again, but I didn't turn around.

"I think you better go." Blanca said.

She twisted her short hair around her finger as she studied his expression.

"She'll be fine." She said in a tone that made it seem as if she was trying to convince herself. "You'll see tomorrow."

He listened to her as he got up and walked over to hug and kiss her before leaving. Blanca closed the door to my room and left to go walk him out.

Less than five minutes later she returned to my room. I didn't move from the bed and she walked back in and cleared her throat. She walked around to the side of the bed that I was laying on and, leaned over, putting her hand to my forehead and brushing back the hair that hung over my cheek.

"You knew what you were getting yourself into." She whispered in my ear harshly and shut off the lights before leaving the room.

Chapter Thirteen

I woke up to the sound of slamming doors as Blanca screamed orders at anyone who got in her way. The moment had arrived. It was the morning of my wedding. I slowly got out of my bed and went to the bathroom to vomit. I was so nervous about the wedding that I couldn't stop myself.

Elena came to my room as I was brushing my teeth and asked if everything was okay. I debated on telling her that I wasn't sure if I could go through with the wedding, but decided not to. It was a good thing that I didn't because Blanca suddenly stormed in.

"Oh my goodness." Blanca wailed when she saw that I was still in my pajamas.

"What is your problem, Ma?" Elena asked obnoxiously.

"I don't have my yellow bangle bracelet."

"What in the world do you need that for?" Elena asked.

"For good luck of course." Blanca responded, with a blank expression on her face.

"Liliana, do you have something blue?" Blanca suddenly asked. "Elena, give the girl something blue. No, then that will be borrowed and it will not count. Liliana, go find something blue that belongs to you."

Blanca appeared frantic. Her hands trembled as she spoke. Elena and I exchanged glances, but I walked around quickly, trying to find something blue.

Blanca's worried mood was soon forgotten as two limousines pulled up outside. We were running late and she hurried us downstairs. The dresses were waiting for us at the church, as were the hair stylists to fix our hair. Blanca shooed us into a limousine, making it seem as if we had no time to spare. The wedding didn't start until three o'clock, but the driver sped to the church per Blanca's orders.

As we pulled up in front of the church, a nun walked out to greet us and guided us to a library in the church where we were to be situated until the wedding began. Elena smiled from ear to ear as she set her things down on the table. A few of the other bridesmaids walked in soon after, followed by Blanca's sister Juana. I didn't know any of them well, but Blanca insisted on them being in the wedding since Antonio had five of his male cousins standing up in the wedding with him.

I glanced around the room nervously as everyone began to greet each other. The library was small, but it fulfilled its purpose. I noticed that there was one empty chair awaiting Madrigal whenever she got there. Blanca had had a seamstress go to my father's house to have her measurements taken for the dress that was hanging across the room on a long rack. I couldn't wait for her arrival so that I would have my own family to talk to.

Two hours passed and Blanca began panicking. Madrigal was not there yet and my father couldn't be reached. Deep inside me, I knew that he would let me down. I felt my stomach begin to do somersaults as we waited for them to arrive.

Blanca called his neighbor's phone over and over again without receiving any response. I sat quietly in my chair as a hairstylist curled my hair.

"He's the type that's usually late." I mentioned to Blanca quietly, hoping that there was still a chance that he would show up.

My fear faded away half an hour later when the hairstylist handed me a mirror to admire the back of my hair. I felt frozen in time for a moment, remembering that everyone else had also been made up and looked around to check out everyone else looked. Everyone looked beautiful. I felt as though I was in a dream. All of my problems were pushed to the past.

Blanca entered the room, appearing exasperated, bringing nervousness back to my bones.

"Madrigal is sick and can't come to the wedding." Blanca moaned as she looked around at everyone's expressions.

"We can't have an empty spot at the wedding. Who is her size that we know?" She asked Elena.

"Oh, I know!" Elena finally said after thinking it over for what felt like hours, "Catalina's youngest daughter, Magalee."

Blanca looked like she was about to have a heart attack. She put her hand to her chest. Her sister, Juana, walked across the room and massaged her left shoulder.

"Is she the only one we know that size?" Blanca asked, shaking her sister off.

"Well unless, you can think of someone better." Elena replied sarcastically.

"I like Catalina's daughters." I said reassuringly.

Blanca glanced at me and raised her eyebrows before she refocused her attention on Elena.

"Call Catalina." Blanca exclaimed as she handed the phone to Elena and finally sat down.

Elena dashed out of the room and ran down the hall to make the call. She mumbled something about checking to see how Antonio and the men were doing. I sat and watched the stylists fixing Roberta and Blanca's hair. The stylist working on Blanca's hair was straightening it layer by layer.

Just then Elena and Magalee walked into the room.

"I was in the area." Magalee said.

Elena laughed. "Catalina's family lives down the street." She explained.

Catalina looked excited as she took off her sweater and her purse on a table.

"Of course, I invited Catalina's whole family to come to the wedding." Elena said to me.

I glanced at her for a moment, feeling confused. "Weren't they already?" I asked.

Elena, Catalina, and I exchanged looks before turning to Blanca, who mumbled something about the cake and then drew her stylist into a conversation. No one muttered another word about the invitations, though I wondered who would be coming to the wedding if not the people I knew.

I didn't have long to think as everyone began to dress me and walked me to a mirror where I stood admiring myself. "Is that me?" I wondered aloud as I stared at myself. It couldn't be. I thought about how much my life had changed in the three short months that I had known Antonio. Where was the girl who was unhappy for such a long time with her father? There was no more waking up at the crack of dawn and going to work for Elena. Now I would be her sister–in–law and a member of her family. I couldn't believe how different I looked as I stood in front of the mirror admiring myself, trying to remember the person that I used to be. My eyes began to water up and I tried hard to fight back tears, but couldn't. Blanca nearly had a heart attack as Elena patted my eyes with tissues.

"Okay, no more mirrors." Blanca said jokingly.

Everyone laughed, including me.

There was a knock at the door and when we opened it a nun stood smiling in at us, with the look of an angel. "It is time." She said as she gripped a gold cross dangling from her neck.

Elena and Roberta fanned themselves nervously as Blanca ushered everyone except me out.

"You come out last." Blanca said to me.

She turned and walked out of the room, stopping and glancing back at me before turning and quickly walking out of the room to the hallway. My wedding party stood waiting for her to instruct them on how to walk down the aisle.

I nervously emerged from the room after I saw the last member of my wedding party slowly walk into the sanctuary. I realized my father wasn't there yet. My heart started to pound heavily. Marcus quietly walked out of the sanctuary and quickly approached me. He said that he would be the one to walk me down the aisle.

Tears welled in my eyes as I held my hand over my face. I felt grateful and nodded to thank him. The music changed and I smiled up at him as I took his arm. He led me down the hallway to the double doors. As we passed through them I knew that this was not only the entrance of the sanctuary, but of my new life. I was about to become Antonio's wife and would vow to love him forever.

I glanced around at the pews as Marcus led me slowly down the aisle. I saw the faces of so many people that I didn't know and then some of the people that I knew to be Antonio's family. None of my own family was there. It made me sad as we continued down the aisle. Everyone was smiling in encouragement as we walked. I smiled back at them, regardless of the fact that I didn't know who many of them were. As we approached the front of the church I stared up at Antonio. He smiled as he stood waiting for me at the end of the aisle. A tear fell from my face, as my attention was directed upon him.

Liliana

He was the love of my life. Suddenly I forgot about why I had been upset with him. Although what happened the day before embarrassed me, I knew that he was the only man in the world that loved me more than life itself. I knew that he would protect me and that I could trust him. Memories of our relationship flooded my mind as I concentrated hard on each step, afraid that I would trip.

Antonio smiled at me warmly as I approached him. I returned the smile as I took my place beside him. The priest motioned for everyone to sit down and began to speak. I did not hear a word that the priest was saying.

I stared at Antonio. He looked so handsome standing before me in a black tuxedo. His chiseled face was tough, yet he stared lovingly at me. His tanned skin was the perfect color and I loved the way his dark curls fell across it. As I stood admiring him, I noticed Antonio's eyebrows rise at me and I smiled blankly as I tried to focus on what the priest was saying.

"Repeat after me, Liliana, in saying I do." I heard the priest say.

I could feel the nerves building up inside of me as I answered and waited for Antonio to be asked the same. I felt like I was in heaven when he finally responded to the priest.

All of my dreams were complete. I had this wonderful man as my husband, I thought to myself as I stood there before him. He was the man who made me the happiest person in the world. He was the man who I knew would bend over backwards for me. I knew that no one would be able to take this happiness away from me as Antonio turned to kiss me for the first time as his wife and our audience cheered for us as we did.

Antonio grabbed my hand as we pulled away from our first married kiss, and led me down the aisle that would lead us to our new life. He reached over and gripped my waist. As we walked out of the church, laughing together, we saw that a crowd had gathered on the stairway waiting to throw rice at us. I felt rice hitting my skin as we laughed again and again and we began to run to avoid being hit by it.

We dove into the back of our limousine and Antonio kissed me so passionately that I wondered if he would be able to stop. His grip on me was tight. He pulled me closer and closer into him. Our kiss was so deep and so passionate that I felt like I couldn't breathe. We were alone in the limousine with the driver, yet I felt like I was being watched and held back slightly, opening my eyes and glancing around to make sure that no one could see us.

The limousine circled the city for what felt like hours. I knew our reception didn't start until two hours after the wedding, but I felt like if we waited that long to get there, we were not going to make it until our wedding night. Antonio climbed on top of me and rubbed his body against mine. I couldn't feel anything because of the ruffled bottom of my wedding dress, but he grunted quietly in between kisses as if he could. He grabbed the dress as though he was going to rip it off, stopping, showing that he was trying his best to contain himself. As I felt my body become wet with desire for him, I felt nervous about how our night would go. He continued to kiss me and gripped my breasts as he did. My body felt like it was on fire as I began to pull him closer to me. Just when I thought that he wouldn't be able to control himself any longer the limousine pulled up outside the reception hall.

"We're here." The driver said as we stopped abruptly.

Antonio and I pulled our lips apart and straightened up our clothing. I reached up and touched my hair. I felt like it was a mess and tried to push my hair back as Antonio's and my eyes met. We smiled mischievously at one another as we attempted to pull ourselves together. He quickly got out of his side of the car and came around to open my door for me.

"I can't wait until tonight." He said to me with a sly grin.

I shot him a worried glance and he grinned, grabbing my hand and leading me to the reception hall quickly, obviously trying to get the party over with as speedily as possible.

There were people lined up outside of the hall as we walked in that we didn't know, shouting their congratulations at us. Antonio held me at his side nervously as he glared at them. Some began to call out questions to him as we passed while others snapped pictures of us. I noticed Gilbert standing at the doorway glaring at the crowd, following us in soon after we passed him, locking the door as we stepped inside.

Anyone that had come in had to have an invitation. There were two people standing at the door verifying that each person's name was on the guest list. Everything seemed to be so organized. I realized how much work Blanca had put into the party and reminded myself to thank her as we walked through the room and toward the door of the banquet hall.

We stood still for a moment, until Antonio caught the DJ's eye and nodded at him.

The DJ asked for everyone's attention and announced us as husband and wife as we entered the room. Everyone inside cheered. Everything felt surreal. Antonio held my hand as we walked to the front of the room, sitting down at our table as he whispered into my ear. I could feel both passion and nervousness growing inside of me as my mind computed what he said. I couldn't believe that this was the night when we would make everything happen. I smiled nervously at our audience as Antonio continued to whisper about dirty things that he wanted to do to me. I blushed and nodded but felt my entire body lock up.

I could feel my panties grow hot and wet as I sat frozen beside him. I didn't know how to react. I felt like everyone knew what he was saying. I nodded and he sat back in his chair and laughed as a server brought over tall glasses of wine and plates of steaming hot entrees. I crossed my legs together tightly as we sat and ate our food and sipped wine while we watched everyone around us.

Antonio devoured his food, while I slowly chewed each piece that I put in my mouth. I wished that I could eat faster, as he began whispering into my ear again as soon as he was finished with his plate.

Antonio called over the waiter and asked him to bring us a bottle of wine. I hadn't even finished my first glass at this point. I felt tense as I picked up my glass and held it to my mouth. I wanted to remember everything that happened at our wedding and wondered if I would. He insisted that I drink more and more in order to relax.

I looked around the room at everyone and figured that I could always watch the video. I gulped down my first glass while he poured another and before long I felt my nipples grow hard within my dress.

I leaned toward him, laughing as we sat looking out at our guests. He took me out to dance and soon our guests came out to the dance floor and danced beside us. Antonio asked a waiter to bring me another glass of wine as we danced and I scolded him about dancing with it because of my white dress but he wasn't listening. He held the glass to my lips and I stopped dancing momentarily to drink it quickly after a few drops fell on my dress. Before long I was clinging to him as our bodies moved, concentrating hard on avoiding stepping on his feet.

When he went underneath my dress hours later to get my garter and throw it out to a crowd of single men, I tried hard not to look surprised as he moved my panties to the side and quickly licked me before coming out from beneath my dress. I felt I was ready for him to penetrate me as I attempted to keep my composure. He smiled at me as he threw the garter out to the crowd and we watched the men fight for it while laughing.

We walked back toward our table when the garter toss was over and I held tightly to him as we walked, out of fear that I would fall. He didn't seem to notice how far gone I was because as soon as we sat down he had someone bring me another glass of wine. I didn't know if I could keep another glass of wine down and shot him a scared expression that made him laugh, but drank it anyway.

I sat stiffly at the table as Miguel and his father came over to talk with us. They each handed Antonio an envelope that he put into his inside pocket and they proceeded to pat his back and shake my hand. I glanced across the room at Elena as the three of them began speaking quickly in Spanish. Elena was attempting to control her children, even though her new nanny was seated beside her. Her daughters had been dancing for hours and now looked like they had become very grouchy as they pulled her hands to leave. I caught her gaze and she smiled and waved, giving me a sign to tell me that I looked beautiful. I smiled back and she went back to attending to them. Suddenly I felt like the room was spinning and leaned on Antonio's shoulder for support as I fell to the side, making it obvious how drunk I was.

Miguel gave Antonio the "thumbs up" sign, and quickly returned to his table. He grabbed one of the girls in his arms and leaned over to whisper into Elena's ear as Antonio Salvador called out for his wife and asked her to have someone bring out the cake. Rather than setting the cake down on the original table that Blanca planned to, she had them bring the cake over to our table and set it down before us, after noticing how gone I was. Antonio helped me up and guided my hand as we cut into it and smiled for pictures. I shook my head as we stood there, but he encouraged me to keep my cool for five more minutes. We entertained the crowd by feeding each other cake with our fingers. He smeared frosting on my nose and I laughed as I tried to get his, missing and wiping it across his cheek, nearly falling over in the process. His mother came over and whispered to us that she would meet us back at our house to help me get my dress off and he nodded happily.

I glanced over at Elena, allowing the fear to show in my eyes as I stared at her. She gave me a sign that said everything was going to be okay. Antonio noticed my expression and rubbed my arm reassuringly, his expression growing more and more excited. We waited for a few minutes before he guided me out the door.

We walked past the cheering crowd and into the limousine where he kissed me continuously as I tiredly kissed him back. He fondled my tender breasts, reaching around me and opening the back of my dress so he could pull the front of my gown down to free them and slip them into his mouth.

I moaned in pleasure as he laid me back in the limousine. He tugged at my dress to get it down past my breasts but the zipper was stuck and wouldn't budge. He pulled my body up and towards him as he furiously kissed me. I felt so sleepy that I didn't realize when we finally pulled up in front of our house. I struggled to get my dress back over my breasts, but it wouldn't stay up. He took off his suit jacket and put it on me.

He helped me out of the car and I clung to him as we began to walk. I felt so tired that I thought I would fall over as we walked slowly toward the door. He anxiously picked me up and carried me inside, kissing me all the while. He didn't stop to close the door, but instead carried me up to our room and laid me on the bed.

I looked wearily across the room to see that Blanca was there in the room as she said she would be. I nearly jumped out of the bed out of fear as she handed a small steak knife to Antonio.

He came at me with the knife.

"What are you doing?" I asked loudly, sitting straight up in the bed.

Antonio pushed me down with one hand and slid the knife under my dress, using it to rip the dress open down the center revealing to him my naked breasts and panties as I shook in fear. He had a look in his eyes that scared me as Blanca removed the dress from beneath me and stepped out of view, turning and walking out to the balcony.

I crossed my hands over my breasts as I stared up at him. Suddenly I felt very awake.

"I wanted to keep that." I murmured as I looked around helplessly at the white walls.

Antonio didn't say anything as he undressed, revealing his strong muscles and fitted boxer shorts. My hands shook as I clung to myself but I couldn't help admiring his nearly naked body. I hadn't realized how big his muscles were and peered at them as sweat glistened on his tan body. The bulge between his legs appeared to be huge and I tried to back away, wanting to scream for help as he climbed on top of me, passionately kissing me and removing my hands from my chest.

He pulled away and looked down at my body, my breasts rising and falling, nipples erect before him as he slyly smiled and began to suck them, cupping and caressing them with his large hands. I felt my insides begin to burn as I grew both nervous and excited about what was about to happen. I wrapped my thin arms around him to pull him closer to me, but he pushed them away, pulling my right hand down to feel his manhood. He moved my hand back and forth as I kissed him as he removed his shorts, repositioning my hand on his naked penis. I fought fear as I tried to focus my attention on him. His manhood seemed to grow bigger as it throbbed in my hand.

"Oh God, Antonio." I said fearfully between our passionate kisses. "I don't think I want to do this."

He laughed as he kissed me harder. I was serious and tried to move away from him with no success. I glanced around the room for help as he sucked my neck. I didn't let go of his manhood as we kissed. I decided that this was a good method of buying time. I held onto it, noticing that it was as hard as a rock and I could feel it pulsating in my hand. He pulled away and smiled at me. I shook my head, I knew what was coming and began to tighten up, out of fear.

He reached down and grabbed the front of my panties so hard that they ripped off, leaving the sides of my legs quivering in pain. I put my hand to his chest again, trying to stop him as he put his finger inside of me. It felt good and it relaxed me as he played with my insides, making me laugh as he touched my pleasure points. He made me wetter than I thought possible, adding two and then three fingers quickly as he kissed me harder. I cried out in pain as he added the third finger, holding my hand to my face to attempt some sort of relief. I tried to push him away, feeling that I couldn't take anymore. He continued to press his fingers inside of me, despite my pleas to stop and spread his fingers open before climbing on top of me and attempting to slip his manhood in. The head slipped in and he stopped momentarily as I cried out in pain loudly.

"Antonio, stop." I struggled to say. "Please stop."

Tears filled my eyes and my body began to shake uncontrollably with fear.

He smiled but held his finger to his lips attempting to silence me. When my shaking and whimpering slowed down he began to move back and forth slowly. I felt like my body would break in half as I again tried to stop him. This time he didn't pull back and just when I thought it couldn't get any worse, he thrust his entire manhood inside me. I screamed out in pain and gripped his back tightly as he paused. This only made him smile as he moaned in pleasure. Tears poured from my face as he began to move faster and faster. I clung onto him tightly, afraid to move and make it any worse. I felt like I was going to die as I felt my vagina begin to drip hot blood. I tried desperately to scoot my body up in the bed, trying to get away from him, but his body followed, pounding into me again and again. He didn't stop for what seemed like hours, as I lay exasperated, gasping and screaming beneath him, tears poured from my face as he held my shoulders so that I couldn't back up.

"Suck my neck." He said loudly through his teeth as he continued to thrust himself into me. "It will help with the pain."

I did as he instructed me and it helped as he worked my body harder and harder. I felt the sweat pouring from both of our bodies. He was so deep inside of me that I felt like he was hitting my organs. I moved my head around to grab his neck several times after losing my grip on it as he continued to speed up. Finally I felt a burst of warmth inside me and he fell to the side, groaning in pleasure.

He released his grip on me and I quickly backed away, trembling as I did.

He stood up moments later and removed the sheet from beneath me, while I rolled to my side holding my body in pain. He called down the hallway to his mother and she came to take the sheet from him, glancing over at me for a moment before leaving. I rolled my naked body up in a fetal position as he talked with her for a moment. I felt like I was going to die. My insides throbbed hard in pain.

He closed the door and came back over to me and held me, running his hands over my body momentarily before rolling me over and starting the whole process again. It was still painful though at this point I didn't fight him. My body seemed to be conforming to his and by the third and fourth round I finally moaned in pleasure with him. He smiled as he looked down at me. My breasts felt like they swelled up against his body.

When we were finally done, I rolled to my side and fell asleep as he stroked my arms and thighs with his left hand.

Liliana

The next morning I woke up early as sunlight beamed in through the white lace curtains. Antonio was not beside me and the sheets were thrown to the side from where he had been sleeping. I wondered if he was in the bathroom but after five minutes or so I realized that the bathroom door was open and there were no noises coming from inside.

I was completely naked but lay there without moving until I saw a white silk robe on a chair nearby. I put it on and luckily I did, because moments later the door opened. The maid came in slowly with a tray of breakfast, glancing around the room as she did. As our eyes met, she quickly left and I began to eat.

Elena came in shortly after. "Are you okay?" She asked, smiling at me coyly.

I rubbed my body and nodded.

"I can't believe that you let my mother do that." She motioned to the balcony and I walked over to it seeing a sheet flailing around in the wind with blood spots on it.

I quickly took it down and rolled it up in a ball, throwing it in the garbage can in disgust.

"Oh no." I exclaimed, holding my hand to my face. "How embarrassing! I didn't realize that happened."

"You didn't know that she did that?" Elena asked.

I shook my head. I sat down and continued to eat my food slowly, without saying a word. What was I supposed to say? Whatever was done was done.

"Where is he?" I asked, I finally asked her.

"Where else?" Elena responded. "At a meeting, where else?"

I sat in frustration for a moment without knowing what to say. I thought Antonio would have stayed there with me. I thought that he would stay with me today or the rest of the week. I shook bad thoughts from my mind as I sat back and she began to talk about the reception. Elena had taken some pictures on her cell phone and I looked through them without remembering taking as many pictures as I had. I must have walked off with her at some part of the night because she had me pictures of me posing in different parts of the banquet hall for her with people that I didn't remember. I hadn't realized that I was that drunk until now.

Antonio came in moments later and shooed Elena out of the room. He quickly came to my side and kissed me. He pulled the sash on my robe and before I knew it, we started going at it again. He didn't give me a chance to question him as he thrust himself inside of me. I moaned loudly in pleasure and he smiled, leaning down to suck on my neck.

"I want a son." He whispered to me. "Give me a son."

He bit down lightly on my neck again, moaning. I felt a blast of warmth inside me and he paused before falling to the side of me. I tried to get up, thinking I needed to take a shower, but he pulled me back down and made love to me again. My insides throbbed in pain as he penetrated me for what felt like hours. My legs felt like they locked to either side of me and it hurt to switch positions as he moved me all over the bed.

While he was inside of me, we didn't talk, I just moaned and grabbed onto his back, as he thrust himself within me. He would smile fiercely with each moan that escaped me. He bit down on my skin from time to time, causing me to moan louder in both ecstasy and pain. Sweat dripped from his body onto me and glistened as it fell across his muscular arms. His chest boasted the perfect amount of hair, just across the middle and top but very thin. I touched it as he made love to me, glancing up at him to take in his expression.

Over the next two months, every moment we spent together went like this. I had little time to eat or to shower when he was around so I tried to get all of my own personal things done while he was at his morning meetings. He wore my body out, making love to me for hours upon hours each day. If I went to the bathroom to try to take a quick shower, he would appear from nowhere and pull my legs around him, holding me in a standing position as he pounded himself powerfully into me and leaned me against the shower wall.

I didn't fight him off and soon it wasn't just him that initiated our lovemaking. It got to the point where as soon as he came in the bedroom door, I was the one attacking him with passionate kisses and guiding him to the bed where he would begin to penetrate me.

He'd told me the day after we were married that he didn't want me to leave the room or even to get dressed until I was carrying his baby and I played along with him. He wanted me to be there, ready for him and those were the rules. I thought of it as a game at first but after a month or so, I was starting to feel like his prisoner.

When Antonio wasn't there, I began to feel sad and lonely. Elena stopped coming over as much because Antonio wanted me to himself when he was there. I told him that I felt like I was being held captive in many ways. He wouldn't listen to me when I told him how I felt. It got to the point that I thought that I would never see the outside world again. I was dependent on him to bring me everything and while I enjoyed living my new luxurious life, I didn't like it at all, at the same time.

After a few weeks feeling sad about it, I became lost in our passionate love affair, living and breathing solely for his touch. It got to the point where he was all I lived for... maybe that was his goal all along.

Book Club Discussion Guide
Liliana
by Neva Squircs-Rodriguez

1. Do you know someone who has been thrown into a 'foreign' situation by circumstance?

2. How could you make a difference for that person?

3. Liliana was just 14 when she traveled to Colombia to live with her father. How did she manage when she didn't even speak the language?

4. How did Liliana help pay off her father's debt?

5. Elena was a friend to Liliana, as well as her employer, but how did the two young women interact when others were around?

6. Elena said her mother had forced her into marriage at just 13. What do you think of very young women marrying? How could a marriage like that be supported so that it would be successful? Could you see yourself married at that age?

7. How did Liliana's father react to his daughter becoming involved with Elena's brother, Antonio?

8. Did Liliana find her knight in shining armor in Antonio?

In Too Deep

Book 2
The Liliana Series

by

Neva Squires-Rodriguez

Prologue

The next morning I woke up early. Sunlight beamed in through the white lace curtains. Antonio was not beside me and the sheets were thrown to the side where he had been sleeping. I wondered if he was in the bathroom but after five minutes or so I realized that the bathroom door was open and there were no noises coming from inside.

I was completely naked but lay there without moving until I saw a white silk robe on a chair nearby. I put it on and luckily I did, because moments later the door opened. The maid came in slowly with a tray of breakfast, glancing around the room as she did. As our eyes met, she quickly left and I began to eat.

Elena came in shortly after. "Are you okay?" She asked, smiling at me coyly.

I rubbed my body and nodded.

"I can't believe that you let my mother do that." She motioned to the balcony and I walked over to it seeing a sheet flailing around in the wind with blood spots on it.

I quickly took it down and rolled it up in a ball, throwing it in the garbage can in disgust.

"Oh no." I exclaimed, holding my hand to my face. "How embarrassing! I didn't realize that happened."

"You didn't know that she did that?" Elena asked.

I shook my head. I sat down and continued to eat my food slowly, without saying a word. What was I supposed to say? Whatever was done was done.

"Where is he?" I asked, I finally asked her.

"Where else?" Elena responded. "At a meeting, where else?"

I sat in frustration for a moment without knowing what to say. I thought Antonio would have stayed here with me. I thought that he would stay with me today or the rest of the week. I shook bad thoughts from my mind as I sat back.

Elena began to talk about the reception. She had taken some pictures on her cell phone and I looked through them without remembering taking as many pictures as I had. I must have walked off with her at some part of the night because she had pictures of me posing in different parts of the banquet hall for her with people that I didn't remember. I hadn't realized that I was that drunk until now.

Antonio came in moments later and shooed Elena out of the room. He quickly came to my side and kissed me. He pulled the sash on my robe and before I knew it, we started going at it again. He didn't give me a chance to question him as he thrust himself inside me. I moaned loudly in pleasure and he smiled, leaning down to suck on my neck.

"I want a son." He whispered to me. "Give me a son."

He bit down lightly on my neck again, moaning. I felt a blast of warmth inside me and he paused before falling to the side. I tried to get up, thinking I needed to take a shower, but he pulled me back down and made love to me again. My insides throbbed in pain as he penetrated me for what felt like hours. My legs felt like they locked to either side of me and it hurt to switch positions as he moved me all over the bed.

While he was inside of me, we didn't talk, I just moaned and grabbed onto his back, as he thrust himself into me. He would smile fiercely with each moan that escaped me. He bit down on my skin from time to time, causing me to moan louder in both ecstasy and pain. Sweat dripped from his body onto me and glistened as it fell across his muscular arms. His chest boasted the perfect amount of hair, just across the middle and top but very thin. I touched it as he made love to me, glancing up at him to take in his expression.

Over the next two months, every moment we spent together went like this. I had little time to eat or to shower when he was around so I tried to get all of my own personal things done while he was at his morning meetings. He wore my body out, making love to me for hours upon hours each day. If I went to the bathroom to try to take a quick shower, he would appear from nowhere and pull my legs around him, holding me in a standing position as he pounded himself powerfully into me and pressed me against the shower wall.

I never fought him off or pushed him away. Soon it wasn't just Antonio that initiated our lovemaking. It got to the point where as soon as he came in the bedroom door, I was the one attacking him with passionate kisses and guiding him to the bed where he would begin to penetrate me.

He'd told me the day after we were married that he didn't want me to leave the room or even to get dressed until I was carrying his baby, and I played along with him. He wanted me to be there, ready for him, and those were the rules. I thought of it as a game at first but after a month or so, I was starting to feel like his prisoner.

When Antonio wasn't there, I began to feel sad and lonely. Elena stopped coming over as much because Antonio wanted me all to himself when he was home. I told him that I felt like I was being held captive in many ways. He wouldn't listen to me when I tried to talk to him about how I felt. It got to the point that I thought that I might never see the outside world again. I was dependent on him to bring me everything and while I enjoyed living my new luxurious life, I didn't like it at all, at the same time.

After a few weeks feeling sad about it, I became lost in our passionate love affair, living and breathing solely for his touch. It got to the point where he was all I lived for... maybe that was his goal all along.

Chapter One

Finally, one Saturday morning, we realized that all of Antonio and my dreams had come true. I woke up earlier than usual feeling nauseous and dizzy. I tapped Antonio's shoulder, belched and then staggered into the bathroom. I felt like I had to throw up, but nothing would come out as I gagged relentlessly as I stood with my head over the bathroom sink. I went to lie back down beside Antonio after the feeling stopped.

Antonio immediately noticed something was wrong. He sat up in bed and stared intently at me. "What's wrong?" He asked, touching my shoulder gently.

I shrugged as I lay beside him. Antonio called for the maid and moments later she brought breakfast up.

"¿Estás bien?" She asked me, as her eyes studied my face. "Ella se ve pálida."

Antonio said something to her that I didn't catch and she came over to the side of the bed and put her hand on my forehead, shaking her head and looking confused as she slowly pulled away. Antonio thanked her and she left our room. I got up and walked to the balcony and lowered myself into a patio chair, figuring the fresh air would help me. The sun was just rising and I could see the sunlight glistening on the blades of grass in our yard.

Antonio carried the tray of food out to the balcony and we sat down to eat. I smiled up at him as he put the tray down in front of me. No sooner did I see the eggs on my plate then I turned to my side and vomited. Antonio quickly rushed over to my side and rubbed my back. I wiped my face with my napkin, feeling as though I had turned green. My first instinct was to run to the bathroom, but my body suddenly felt so weak that I didn't think I could move.

"Baby, are you okay?" He asked worriedly.

I shook my head, though I couldn't talk. I still felt like vomiting and did several times off the side of the balcony as he watched with a disgusted look on his face. He came over after the second time to hold my hair and rub my back as I vomited acid out of the depths of my stomach. I grabbed onto him after the vomiting fit ceased and he helped me sit back down in the chair. I wiped sweat from my forehead as a smile appeared on his face.

"Lilly, your monthly friend hasn't visited at all since we've been married." Antonio exclaimed suddenly.

I sat in shock for a moment as I thought about it.

"No." I replied. "Actually it hasn't."

No sooner did I say confirm what he had said, then Antonio had a smile on his face from ear to ear. He picked me up and carried me to the bed.

"I'm going to be a papa!" He exclaimed.

"Quiet. Please Tony, don't get excited yet." I said quietly. "I mean we don't know for sure."

"No." He replied loudly. "I know for sure. I have a feeling about this. I'm calling the doctor."

He picked up his cell phone and called his mother for the doctor's number and avoided her questions, saying that he would call her back later. He quickly dialed the doctor and ordered him to come over immediately, saying that he didn't care how much it cost him. A second later he ran out onto the balcony.

"I'm going to be a Papa." He screamed, leaning over the side, looking like he would lose his balance and fall.

"Oh my goodness." I said putting my hand over my face, blushing.

One of the gardeners shouted out his congratulations to Antonio as they talked back and forth. Minutes later the doctor pulled into the driveway and Antonio ran out of the room and down the stairs to bring him up to our room. Antonio pushed him along as he entered the room with him moments later. Antonio stayed in the room while the doctor examined me, becoming nervous as the doctor took his time to give him his opinion.

"Congratulations." The doctor said, confirming the answer that Antonio had been waiting for. "She is about six weeks along."

Antonio immediately jumped up and hugged him. I smiled as I watched Antonio. He looked as though he had received the best news in the world. I was excited, but I thought Antonio was much more excited than I was. I asked him not to tell anyone that I was pregnant until I was at least halfway through the pregnancy.

"Why?" He asked, with a childish look on his face.

"I don't know." I replied. "I'm just nervous, I guess."

I felt kind of embarrassed, I knew everyone knew that we were married, but now they would know that we had sex. I just wasn't used to talking about things like that. I remembered when I had my first period, I didn't even tell my mother about it, she found out on her own a week later when she was doing the laundry. I was only eleven and she had been planning to talk to me about menstruation when I was twelve, thinking that I wouldn't have my first period until I was thirteen like she did.

Antonio paced the room but paid little attention to me as he called his mother to tell her to have everyone come to the house for a barbeque that afternoon. I sighed, knowing that he would not be able to contain the news and asked him if I could have my clothes back. He took me across the hall to another bedroom where all of our clothes were in the closet. This room had a larger bathroom and its balcony overlooked the backyard. He told me we would stay in that room from that point on in our marriage as he happily showed me where everything was.

The room boasted deep colors of brown and red. The sheets on the bed felt silky and smooth as I ran my hand down them. I grabbed him and tried to pull him close to me for a kiss, but he pulled my hand and led me out to the balcony where he had the maid bring up some crackers and ginger ale for me. Antonio and I sat out on the balcony for a few hours letting everything sink in before realizing that we had to get ready for the barbeque.

"Everyone should be here soon." He said. "Do you need help getting ready?"

I shook my head and got up slowly, going inside and removing my robe he watched me. I took a hot shower as he stood at a distance, handing me soap and shampoo so that I wouldn't have to bend down to lift it up. He held out a towel for me, drying me up as I came out. I put on comfortable clothing and my stomach clenched as I reached down to put on my gym shoes.

"Do you need me to tie your shoes?" He asked.

"No, Tony. I'm fine." I replied.

His excitement was getting me excited. I did feel like I needed a few minutes to myself, to let the baby news sink in. When he began getting ready, I took the opportunity to think about what was going on. I felt the shock sinking in. I couldn't believe that I had a baby growing inside of me. I rubbed my stomach, as I thought about it. Antonio noticed and came to my side and hugged me.

"My baby's having my baby." He said.

I closed my eyes in an attempt to cherish the memory forever. This was the happiest moment of my life. I felt happier than the day that we were married, or the day that I had met him. I had always wondered what it would be like to become a mother, soon I would know.

I leaned against him and he put his hand on my stomach as we sat down on the bed. He laid me back on the bed slowly and kissed my stomach lightly. He hugged me as we lie side by side and then lightly began to move his fingers through my hair. I closed my eyes and he kissed my eyelids.

"Are you tired baby?" He asked and stroked my eyelids softly until I fell asleep.

I didn't think I was tired but suddenly I felt exhausted. I tried to lift my arm to hold him but it just fell to the side. I felt weak as I lay beside him, falling into a light sleep.

After what felt like only a few minutes, the doorbell rang. Antonio got up quietly, and left the room. I slowly rolled to my side and got out of bed. I put on a little makeup in and then walked slowly downstairs. As I walked down the stairs I noticed that Antonio was handing out cigars to our guests. As I made my way down the stairs, they smiled and Antonio came to my side to help me.

"Here she is." Antonio exclaimed. "My beautiful wife and my child in waiting."

Everyone cheered again and began coming over to hug me and kiss my cheek. I must have turned beet red, I was so embarrassed.

"I know you didn't want me to say anything, Lilly." Antonio called out, "but I couldn't help it."

"Aye, you're going to be a papa mijo!" Marcus said as he put his arm around Antonio's shoulder and led him outside.

Roberta quickly came and began asking me questions about my pregnancy. I spoke with her as Blanca glanced at us from across the room with an expression that made me question how she felt about the pregnancy.

Minutes later Antonio was back at my side. He went out of his way to make me comfortable. He even insisted on feeding me steak tacos and rice by hand. I was hoping that he would calm down about the pregnancy, but as the day progressed he didn't. Blanca even yelled at him and told him that he was smothering me as he patted my face down with a napkin after seeing me miss my mouth with my cup.

"Shut up woman." He replied to her jokingly.

Blanca didn't look like she took the joke well and ended up avoiding me the rest of the night. Elena couldn't stop smiling at me. She told me how excited she was at the thought of becoming an aunt. I had begun to become excited about the pregnancy after everyone left. Antonio and I curled up in bed as soon as the last guest had left and we talked about the excitement that we were both feeling. We talked for at least ten minutes, before I decided to climb on him and kiss him. He pushed me back immediately and turned on the television.

"Let's watch a movie," was his response.

"Okay." I said laughing, thinking he was joking and began kissing his neck.

He pushed me away again, this time roughly and I became upset.

"What's wrong?" I asked as I wiped loose strands of hair from my face. I wasn't used to getting this kind of a reaction from him. Every night since we'd been married, we had taken advantage of our marriage, kissing and making love all night long. Tonight he wanted to watch television. I didn't get it.

"I can't make love to you." He said apologetically. "Now I know that my baby is in there."

He began to rub my stomach and smile. I folded my arms across my chest and stared angrily at him. He turned back to the television and used the remote to begin flipping channels as I sat up straight on the bed. Was this how it was going to be? I wondered. I stared at him as my nostrils flared heavily.

"It didn't stop you last night." I retorted after a moment.

"I didn't know last night." He replied, without looking at me.

I leaned back against the pillows and sulked. Would he be like this during my whole pregnancy I wondered? I felt extremely sad. I sat there as he watched television intently and suddenly I felt unattractive. A tear ran down the left side of my face as I sat staring blankly at the television. I noticed a several tattoos on his back that I had never seen before and questioned him about them. He sighed and turned to me, kissing me on the side of my wet cheek.

"Lilly, I'm tired." He said to me. "Can we go to sleep?"

He reached over me and turned off the light, without waiting for an answer. I lay there in shock for a while. What had just happened? I felt completely rejected. He didn't even try to hold me as we attempted to go to sleep. When I finally relaxed a little, he reached over and began to rub my stomach again. I felt animosity grow toward him until I fell asleep.

The next morning he had to go to a meeting and kissed me on the cheek before running out the door of our room. This was not my first morning having breakfast alone, but suddenly I felt more alone than ever. I played with my food for a while and drank my orange juice. Everything looked disgusting to me. I knew that I wouldn't be able to keep it down so I didn't even try to eat it. A couple minutes later the juice came up.

I ran to the bathroom and vomited again and again into the to the white toilet bowl. I swished water around in my mouth and tried to regain my composure. I felt horrible. I finally had my clothes and could walk all over the house and all that I wanted to do was fall over and lay down in the bed. I called up Elena as I did just that and told her how I was feeling. I cried into the phone and within an hour she came over with her son. Elena rubbed a cool cloth on my head as I moaned.

"What's wrong with me Elena?" I moaned. "I feel so horrible. Is this normal?"

"Every pregnancy is different." She said to me. "I never felt that badly, but it doesn't mean that it's not normal."

She stayed with me the rest of the day. Antonio came home in the afternoon and then left again after seeing that she was caring for me. He didn't return until later that night after it was dark and everyone had left. I was too tired to ask him where he had been. He didn't offer an explanation as he slipped into bed beside me. He put his hand gently on my stomach again and fell asleep.

I was confined to my bed for the next month and a half. This time it was my own choice. I was so sick that I felt like I needed to stay near my bathroom at all times. The doctor came to check on me twice before my three month appointment, but said that there was nothing wrong and that it was just an effect of the pregnancy. Antonio and his family were worried about me because I began to lose weight, rather than to gain it and became incredibly weak.

One morning at the beginning of my second trimester I woke up feeling extremely hungry. I called down to the maid and she immediately brought up breakfast. I quickly ate everything on my plate and when nothing happened, I called Elena to let her know that food had finally stayed down. After hanging up with her, I asked the maid to bring me more immediately. She smiled at me and told me that she could see the color returning to my face.

After eating a third full plate, I took a shower and got dressed. I felt excitement grow as I left my room. I glanced down the hallway and quickly walked down the stairs to explore my house, something that I hadn't yet had the opportunity to do. I knew that Antonio was at a meeting so I didn't bother to call him to tell him that I was feeling better. I knew that he would be home around lunchtime anyhow.

I was so happy to finally leave our room that I went into our kitchen to say hello to the maids. They didn't seem happy to see me in their space, so I quickly left the room. I stopped in our spacious living room and noticed that a huge portrait of Antonio and me hung on the wall. I didn't remember seeing it before and was a little upset that Antonio never brought it upstairs to show me the picture. I sat down directly in front of it and sat starring at it for a while I snacked on a banana that I had grabbed while passing through the kitchen. One of the maids came in and brought me lunch without saying a word as she glanced at me nervously. I shrugged off her behavior and ate my food as I began to wonder where Antonio was. Had he been coming home for lunch after we found out about my pregnancy? I honestly didn't know because I had spent the majority of my time in bed sleeping.

I ate alone and when I was finished the maid came and took my plate and asked if I would like anything else. I shook my head as I wiped my hands off on a napkin. I walked across the room to a table with a landline and called Antonio's cell phone but he didn't answer. I gazed around the room for a while longer, before getting bored. Elena had been busy when I called and said she would call back but hadn't yet. I wondered if I should call her back or wait. I couldn't believe that after being cooped up in my room for so long, it was possible for me to become bored. I sighed and stood up, deciding that I would explore the other rooms in the house.

At the bottom of the stairs, I found Antonio's study. I went to sit down on a brown leather chair behind his desk and looked at numerous pictures of him and other family members. I noticed that one picture frame was face down on a small table at the corner of the room and went over to pick it up. It was a picture of me. I remembered that Elena had taken that picture of me the day of her daughter's party. I picked it up so that my face was facing him whenever he sat at his desk and wondered if one of the maids had turned it over, or if it had simply fallen down. I bit down on my bottom lip as I looked around the room.

I stood up and walked across the room to a bookshelf noticing that there were a few books written by Jane Austen. I remembered reading several of them with my mother as a child. I picked up one and sat down on a sofa that was in the room and began to read it. After an hour, I tried to call Antonio again, but still there was no answer and I began to get worried. I looked out the window, trying to find something unusual about the day and after a minute had passed I sat back down on the sofa, leaning back and without warning, fell asleep.

"Hey, what are you doing in here?" I heard Antonio ask as I slowly opened my eyes. "Are you feeling better?"

I nodded, glancing over at a clock on the wall, only to see that it was already four thirty.

"I'm sorry I'm so late." He said as he walked across the room and kissed me. "The meeting took longer than expected. What did you do today?"

I saw him glance at the table with my picture as he sat down at his desk. He nervously fiddled with a pen as he waited for my response.

"Nothing," I replied. "I missed you."

Antonio quickly waked across the room, hugged me and gave me a long kiss.

"Let's go upstairs," he suggested.

I smiled as he led me upstairs. Instead of taking me to our room as I hoped, he took me to the room across the hall. He motioned for me to follow him in.

"I figured this could be the baby's room." He said. I looked disappointed as he began rattling off plans.

"What's wrong?" He asked. "We could knock down a wall if it's too small and we'll need to paint it, but I figured we won't do that until we know if it's a boy or a girl."

I shook my head as my eyes filled with tears.

"Oh Tony, that's not it," I replied. "I want you to make love to me. I feel like you think I'm hideous or something. You never touch me anymore."

Antonio sighed and shrugged at me as I stood before him, putting my hand to my face to hold back tears.

"Would that make you happy?" He asked playfully.

I nodded and smiled as I looked up at him.

"Ok." He replied. "I know have been neglecting my beautiful wife, so let's do this."

I grinned and we walked hand in hand across the hall to our room. I stripped off my clothes sexily in front of him as he smiled and took off his tie. I was down to my bra and panties when his cell phone rang. I felt my heart drop as he looked down at it before glancing back at me. I shook my head and tried to pull him to the bed.

"I have to get this." Antonio said apologetically. "Just get ready for me and I'll be off in a minute."

He answered the phone and I walked across the room, climbing into bed and removing my last articles of clothing as he stepped out of the room to have his conversation. A second later he came back in.

"I'm sorry baby, but I have to go." He said.

Tears welled in my eyes and I nodded and turned away. He sat down next to me and rubbed one of my shoulders and leaned over to kiss the other. I felt humiliated as I sat down on the bed naked before him.

"I'm sorry, but now with the baby coming, I need all the business I can get. I promise I'll make it up to you when I get home." He said.

I nodded without turning to him. He hugged me, put some cologne on and then left the room.

I slowly put my clothes back on and walked over to the window in our old room to watch him leave. I waved as if he could see me and then went to lie down on our old bed. For a few minutes, I just layed there and enjoyed the breeze. The sheer white curtains blew in the wind. As I lay there, I could feel my eyelids growing heavier and fell into a deep sleep. I didn't wake up again until the middle of the night. I was startled to still be in our old room and wondered why he hadn't woke me when he came home.

My stomach began to growl with hunger and I called out quietly for Antonio in the dark. When I didn't hear a response, I silently walked over to the window and saw that his car was there, along with Gilberts. I walked across the hall to our room but he wasn't there. I put on my robe and left the room, going to the front stairway to look for him when I heard his voice downstairs. I knew immediately that he was in the study talking with Gilbert as both their jackets were hung on the coat rack. I crept down the back stairway and snuck into the kitchen to make us both a snack.

I was very careful to be quiet because I didn't want Charles to wake up and offer to do it for me or to see me in my robe for that matter. I found a tray and loaded it with all kinds of goodies. Then I filled up two glasses with juice and carried everything on the trays down the hall toward the study. I smiled when I saw Gilbert sleeping in a chair nearby. I opened the door to the study by pushing it with my butt, not realizing that I had just heard Antonio talking with someone a few moments before and unaware that someone could be with him, beside Gilbert.

I turned as I walked in and to my horror, Antonio was standing with his eyes closed and his pants down to his knees as he leaned against the desk and was getting a blow-job from a red haired woman. His hand sat on top of my picture, which he had laid down upon the desk. I gasped and dropped the tray. They both turned around and I backed up only to realize that I had lost feeling in my legs and fell backwards onto my buttocks.

"Owe," I cried out in pain as multiple pains shot through me.

Gilbert woke up and quickly jumped up to see what was going on. Antonio who was still zippering up his pants came out to help me and immediately started yelling at Gilbert.

"You were supposed to give me a warning, man!" Antonio shouted at him.

"Unbelievable! Do I pay you to sleep?" Antonio said as he looked from side to side, not knowing what to do or to say to me as I sat with my head covered in tears.

Gilbert didn't say anything and I could hear Charles coming out of his room. Antonio leaned down and tried to hold me, but I backed away from Antonio quickly and fell to my side. My tears were uncontrollable, but I tried to sit up and yell at Antonio.

"How could you?" I managed to get out of my throat.

Charles came running toward us with his robe on, seeing the red head and exchanging looks with Antonio. Antonio backed away from me putting his hand over his forehead and not knowing what to say. The redhead seemed to be gathering her things from the room and stopped to put my picture back upright on his desk.

"What happened?" She asked Antonio, but he said nothing as he handed the red head her coat and told Gilbert to take her home.

"Don't move." She said to me. "You need a doctor."

"Owe." I cried out again in pain and tried to sit up again, determined not to listen to her.

"Antonio how could you?" I yelled with all the force that I could muster. "We're married."

As I yelled, I grasped my stomach in pain and felt a heavy rush between my legs. Antonio turned very pale as he starred down at me. I sobbed hard into my hands and looked around at everyone who had suddenly become quiet.

"What?" I asked them.

"You-You're bleeding." Antonio said to me.

I looked down and saw that the middle of my robe was covered in blood.

"No." I shook my head and softly said. "No."

I tried to stand up but could feel myself falling to the side, without being able to stop myself. I felt my face hit the floor hard and can remember pain rushing through my body. I fainted. When I woke up again I was in a hospital room with Antonio who was waiting for me to wake up. His eyes were wet from crying and he held my hand tightly. As soon as everything came into focus and I remembered what had happened, I quickly pulled my hand away. He immediately began to apologize.

"My baby," I said weakly, not listening to him as he talked."

I grabbed his hand again and pulled it toward me.

"The baby is ok?" I asked.

He shook his head as he stared apologetically at me.

"No." I said and began to cry as I snatched my hand back from him.

He tried to console me, putting his arms around me as he tried to hug and kiss me, but I pushed him away over and over again until he stopped. I sobbed to myself with him standing over me. When I finally pulled myself together I looked him right in the eye, my eyes full of rage.

"I want a divorce." I said, gritting my teeth as I spoke to him.

He shook his head.

"Not going to happen." He replied, this time his voice filled with anger. "There will be more chances for children."

"No." I said just as angrily. "That's not it. Do you think that I don't remember what happened, Tony?"

"I saw you. How could you?" I asked him.

"I said that I was sorry." He said briskly.

"Is that it? Do you think that's going to make it better Tony?" I asked.

I sat still quietly for a moment before shaking my head.

"I want a divorce." I said again.

"No." He said, his voice beginning to fill with rage. "That will never happen. I would kill you before I allowed that. Don't test me Lilly."

He walked across the room, scaring me as his nostrils flared. He picked up a table and threw it across the room. I jumped, but did not let it scare me enough to remain quiet.

"In our religion there is no such thing as divorce." He said.

"Bullshit!" I screamed, my own words surprising me as they came out. "You were unfaithful to me. I hate you Tony."

"I was not." He screamed back. "I never had sex with that woman."

"Oh, so you just had your dick in her mouth?" I screamed back at him, my chest filling with pain.

"That's not the same!" He said.

"Oh my God!" I said quietly before going into a screaming fit. "Oh my God, Antonio. Do you really expect me to believe that?"

I picked up a phonebook that was on the table beside me and threw it at him.

"How could I ever be with you again?" I screamed at him angrily.

"Think about it." He replied and grit his teeth. "I am the only one that cares about you."

I sat silently as my heart seemed to drop into my stomach.

"What are you going to do if you leave me?" He asked without waiting for an answer. "You have nothing?"

I sat quietly for a moment and glanced out the window across the room. His words felt like a knife as they seemed to stick the inside of my chest. I felt as if I couldn't breathe as I sat before him.

"You, care about me?" I got out in a low voice and looked over at him.

He nodded as he walked back toward the bed.

"Come on now Antonio." I said, my voice raising as I spoke.

I looked down at my hands and then up at him.

"You chose a really bad way to show it." I yelled across the room at him, as a nurse walked into the room.

"Can you please keep it down in here?" She said briskly. "This is the recovery unit."

She suddenly realized who Antonio was and apologized and walked out of the room.

"Call Elena." I ordered him.

"No." He replied quickly.

"Not until you calm down, besides she's probably sleeping at this time." He said as he glanced down at his watch.

"Well get over it because I'm not calming down." I snarled at him. "I need her, not you."

"Lilly calm down." He said sternly.

"No." I replied. "You're not my father."

"Oh and do you think that if I was your father, your life would be so much better?" He asked. "I'm your husband and I said to calm down."

"You're not much of a husband." I spat out at him, hardly getting the words out of my mouth.

He stood over me and slapped me hard across the face. He backed away and immediately apologized.

"Get out of here." I screamed, my face tingling in pain.

I saw the nurse walk by and instead of coming in to help she shut the door. I began sobbing. Who was I kidding? This was my life and this was how it went. I cried so hard that I started choking and sat up. When I did he held me. I tried to pull away from him, but there was no use. I collapsed in his arms choking on my tears as he began to rub my back. I could feel him crying with me and this only made anger shoot through my body. He stroked my hair and whispered into my ear.

"I'm sorry." He said again and again.

I didn't respond to him as he spoke. I'm sorry doesn't cut it I thought to myself. How could he have put me in this position? How could I have put myself in this position? In all honestly, I hardly knew him before we got married. I wondered what my mother thought of me as she looked down from the heavens. My life was such a failure. I felt hurt and betrayed. On top of everything else, I was so sad for losing my baby and confused because I still loved this horrible man with all of my heart. I pulled away and gazed up at him with sad eyes.

"I need some time apart." I said softly, holding my hand out and touching his chin. "I think I'll ask Elena if I can stay with her for a while."

"No," Antonio replied. "How would that look?"

"Is that all you care about?" I asked. "It will look even worse if word gets out that I want a divorce."

I sighed as I looked around the room.

"You can tell everyone that I am staying with her until I recover." I said softly. "No one has to know why I'm really there."

He shook his head again in disbelief but thought about it for a while as he sat across from me. Finally he nodded and agreed to go along with it. He apologized again and quickly left the hospital room without looking back at me.

I didn't need to call Elena. She showed up to come and get me about an hour later. Elena was sad for the loss of the baby but she said she was thrilled at the thought of me moving in for a while. I knew that she felt lonely with Miguel, just as I did with Antonio. We lived a different type of life. It was a life that couldn't be claimed as our own. We left the hospital in silence that morning.

Author Neva Squires-Rodriguez

Neva Squires-Rodriguez was born and raised in a neighborhood located on the North Side of Chicago. Mother, Wife, Expert at Multitasking... and now, Author, Neva creates electrifying stories with a twist.

Neva Squires-Rodriguez earned her Masters Degree from National University, a feat which she worked very hard to obtain and says she will work even harder to pay off.

She claims to be a typical American, full of dreams that will hopefully get her to a more comfortable lifestyle one day. She says, "God has a plan and I will follow wherever it is that He takes me."

Where to find Neva Squires-Rodriguez online

Website: http://NevaSquiresRodriguez.com
Twitter: @NevaRodriguez22
Facebook: https://www.facebook.com/pages/Neva-Squires-
Rodriguez/1497271613835645
Blog: http://NevaSquiresRodriguez.com

VANILLA HEART PUBLISHING